WHOLE WORLDS
Could
PASS AWAY

Collected Stories

WHOLE WORLDS *Could* PASS AWAY

Collected Stories

Rickey Gard Diamond

Rootstock Publishing

First Printing: July 2017

WHOLE WORLDS *COULD* PASS AWAY
Copyright © 2017 by Rickey Gard Diamond
All Rights Reserved.

ISBN-10: 1578690005
ISBN-13: 978-1578690008
Library of Congress Control Number: 2017941734

Published by Rootstock Publishing
an imprint of Multicultural Media Inc.
www.rootstockpublishing.com
info@rootstockpublishing.com

Email the author at rgdiamond@comcast.net

Cover and book design by Carrie Cook
yoka_vermont@yahoo.com

Printed in the USA

WHOLE WORLDS *Could* PASS AWAY
TABLE OF CONTENTS

BLACK BEARS

She'd not remembered the bear for decades, until a day it was useful. But the memory had hunkered down near her brain stem, where fear and teeth live. When a girl, she had made it a habit to sit on the old, long-dead bear, its mouth open on the floor of her grandfather's library, its ears moth-eaten.

She'd been told that when the family first built the farmhouse where she grew up, black bear were easy to come by. Bear grease had kept their boots waterproofed and guarded their iron gears from rust, and the meat had lasted a long time, sickening sweet except in small portions. The bears seen since then, when Grandpa was a boy, were hardly worth the trouble of hunting, not like the big one there in front of the wood stove. She didn't know how old that bear must have been, older than Grandpa.

Brick suburbs had encroached on the bears' woods by then, the farmhouse uncoupled from the farm. She never saw a live bear until a class trip to the Lincoln Park Zoo. That bear had tucked into himself to sleep with back toward them, disappointingly plump and humped and mild, not like the fanged one back home. It sprawled out footless with four legs flat, its belly flat, too.

She loved to feel her belly against his back, stroking his fur, which, though dry, remained oily enough to leave a dusty coating on her hands that smelled musty. She felt a pleasure fierce as her fear when she wiped hands clean on her clothes afterward. Only soap worked to rid her of what she imagined death must feel and smell like, yet she could never wait for the sink. First she'd rub the warmth of her thigh through her jeans, her muscle. She had touched the golden glass eyes of the bear, the ivory fangs and hard tongue, and the animal lay silent, unblinking.

Her cousins, Doug and Denny, used to scare her with the bear whenever they came over. They'd put their hands under its jaw and raise its head to make it snarl at her. She shouldn't have been scared, but she was, and they knew it. They'd chased her with it one time, wearing it like a cape until they were caught by their grandpa.

Her cousins wore holsters and had caps for their guns, cowboy hats and one sorry pair of spurs that had broken. They fought over them, jingling, until one of them had the idea of giving the broken pair to her, so she could play too. But mostly she pretended to be a wild mustang. They could never catch her, so after only a short run they lost interest. They had their brother-rivalries to maintain.

"Can so."

"Cannot."

"Can so."

"Cannot, lemme see you."

She was supposed to be playing with her doll house, but its plastic figures stood straight with their arms at their sides, never smiling or crying, and too tiny. She made them talk to each other, and sometimes they got into fights, bumping their bodies with sound effects, like the ones Grandpa read her in the Sunday Comics. Biff, bam, ba-boom. It made her grandmother come in and ask what she was doing.

"That's not the way to play with your dolls," she'd say. "I think they want to have a tea party, don't you? What did you do with that pretty china set Santa gave you?" Sometimes Grandma would make Doug and Denny have a tea party with her, but they were only expected to put up with it for a minute or two. "Duke is barking, come on. Last one out's a rotten egg."

She couldn't run outdoors in winter weather without stopping to put on her snow pants under her dress, and by then Doug and Denny were gone. She rather liked it when they were gone. She was sick of their contests. That's what she told herself.

⁂

They all grew up, and Denny, who was younger than Doug, finally won their rivalry. Doug had tested out 4-F for the draft, found out as nearly deaf—probably the reason he'd done poorly in school, everyone said, trying to make him feel better. Denny showed no such mercy, dare, double-dare you. As soon as he was 18, he signed up for the marines so he could go straight to Nam.

The marines were in the front lines, the toughest, everyone said. The family had a party and Denny wore his uniform, and Doug stayed at a distance, quiet. When it was time for Denny to go, Doug gave him a soft punch in the shoulder, saying, "You go get'em."

Three months later, Denny stepped on a mine, exploded to death. Everyone said they couldn't believe it, not even when the body came home; they kept the casket shut. Doug got quieter, off by himself. He lived with his mom, though he had a job at the garage, and this was way past the time when people thought he ought to get married and carry on the family name.

The family name didn't matter for her. She'd already given that up, married at 19, hoping to save the young boy she'd been dating from the draft. He already had his number. She ought to have started in sooner having babies. That's what she told herself. But the war had gotten worse, and she only discovered she was pregnant after he went straight to Nam. She let him down, having a girl-baby in war-time. She sent him a picture of their girl on the bear rug, hoping he'd laugh. She looked darling, but scary next to those teeth.

The war went on and on, as if it would never stop. She read about it and even began to think the students from Kent State might have been within their rights, protesting the war, although she wished more people would support the soldiers when they came home. It was awful, this killing coming so close. Soldiers had gone and shot kids on campus, but the soldiers were nothing but kids, she saw, because by then she'd birthed a boy herself, and it seemed if the war grew long enough, he might go straight to Nam next.

She voted in the next election, keeping it secret that her vote canceled out her husband's, who was still overseas, determined we should win any war that we entered. She was sick of this war, sick of what she saw on the news every night. What chance had Denny ever had in those jungles? There were dozens of others whom she knew, equally dead. Those who remained alive had parts of themselves missing, sometimes feet or fingers, sometimes a heart, a light in the eye, dead as that black bear for all of their teeth-baring. What chance would her own boy have?

Her husband made it home from the war. He sat silent, almost as silent as Denny, as silent as Doug. There wasn't enough left of him to care about their children, or about carrying on the family name, or much of anything. He had been a medic, but didn't want to talk about it.

Then President Johnson stepped down and there was a mess in Chicago, everyone mad at everyone, so that Nixon ended up on top of the stack and the war kept on, coming closer to home now in other ways. She read with mixed excitement and fear about Medgar Evers and Malcolm X, both brave and both killed, on top of the second Kennedy, and then Martin Luther King. Biff, bam, ba-boom. She didn't count up all those murdered men, the ones who had talked about dreams, until that day she was useful. Her memories of this had only blurred and sunk into something dark and frightening that became the floor of her life.

She tried not to care when they caught Kissinger in Cambodia and the papers leaked out of the Pentagon, and finally the men in charge grudgingly went to Paris for peace talks, because at least they still had their Cold War to prove things. All of this stayed jumbled underfoot, her own life mostly concerned with making ends meet and feeding her two kids healthy food and sewing them matching red plaid outfits for Christmas portraits, which she gave to what was left of the family. Some parts weren't talking to other parts by now, opinions about the war heated. Mostly it was the women who tried to talk.

Her aunt said one Christmas about this time that her son looked an awful lot like Denny had when he had been that age. Her mom added quickly, "And like his dad, too," because he had come home alive at least, though he sat unmoved by any memory he could share. She longed for some difference she couldn't describe.

She worked up nerve to divorce her husband after Nam was over, worn out by his never talking, his not liking her anymore, or much of anything. She went to school, she got a job, she met a guy who had never gone to Nam. Her kids hated him; then her kids hated her. They felt sorry for their dad, who was more a man than the man she'd fallen in love with, who played music and talked a lot, and whose family had real china for real tea parties, and who thought the war in Nam had been run by knuckleheads.

His family fought with words all the time. Biff, bam, ba-boom. They talked and talked and nobody won because nobody lost. That wasn't the point; talking was. She decided that, however behind the times she might be, she would make love, not war. She and her new husband had great sex, including the weekend they went to Washington, D.C. on business, combining work with pleasure. Britain's new prime minister was in town, her purse in hand, meaner than any men in Britain, and visiting with the actor who by then was the President.

From their hotel room, she watched Her Honorable Mrs. on television news, proof that women had been liberated, at last able to race as fast as boys all the way to the Falklands. It was enough to make her wonder if the women's movement had been all that good a thing. Maybe none of the commotion over women and segregation had meant much of anything that would make a real difference. She had noticed every black person she saw in her nation's capital was cleaning halls with mops, or standing on corners, asking for coins.

All the suited people, white as she was, hurried for

appointments, looking worried they were late. A careerist herself now, she took up the feeling, walking faster, hiding her mood's darkness, which told her unless she hurried up and worked harder, she'd be poor again.

She and her husband could afford this time together because they were here on business and could legally deduct it from their taxes, paid to protect their nation's privilege of winning whatever war they were in. Losers could not expect pleasures, and her pleasure was useful to what happened later. Sex would soften her cells, change dry bone fear into cartilage and blood. It would leave her mitochondria dancing, ready for shape-shifting.

Afterward, she and her husband went to visit the memorial that had been in all the news. The one designed by a woman, young and Asian, which gave her some hope that maybe some things could change, had changed. She wanted to see the thing. She wanted to see Denny's name there on the wall.

The black of the stone was vast and polished and flat and angled to pierce the earth and sink itself and all who saw it. She stood in front of its shining panels with hundreds of other people, gazing up at dulled engraved names, all the war dead spelled out, every man and woman who had gone straight to Nam, who had come home, here to a black wedge that broke the ground and opened buried hearts who saw it. She didn't want to cry, surprised by the urge. She barely remembered Denny as a young man; there hadn't been much life lived when his had ended. She still thought of him as boy. He had been a boy.

Her own boy was in Macedonia, carrying a gun called a peacekeeper, as she stood there. Over my dead body, she had said to him about his enlisting, and he had signed up anyway, and now dressed in camouflage. He would learn skills in the army, most of them about killing, and now he was a man. His father didn't say this, nor did her son, but this was how manhood proved itself, by what it never had to say. Her cousin Doug knew that, too, without ever having to see Denny's name spelled out on stone.

Her boy would try to win the same rivalry: cannot, can so, cannot, can so. A bunch of knuckleheads, that's what she told herself, but it wouldn't help for her to say so. Only boys who ran in their races could say it to have it mean anything, she thought. She stood there, surprised by all she faced here: sorrow, helplessness, frustration, rage.

She stood at the wall and recalled a news report she had read not long before this and, unbidden, the story from Yosemite returned. Bears, dark as this marble, had made their rounds to raid trash cans at night, becoming so common, so present, that people no longer took them seriously—as if their feet were footless, their spineless backs splayed out in some living room. Until one bear had come rippling on its blades of gliding shoulder, and they heard the woman in her sleeping bag, screaming, "Oh dear god!" Parts of her were eaten, missing until they shot the beast, who had only been hungry and tired of garbage.

A hollow inside her echoed, ohdeargod. Parts of her eaten and missing at this black marble wall, one bear tumbling out, its teeth locked with an older bear of flattened death and dry girlhood. Pleasure had moved her blood earlier, had flexed her heart and, now emptied by the glassy eyes of grief all around her, she smelled that gaping mouth of memory, and she wept.

Her new husband, guilty of living, looked grateful for the chance to put his arm around her huddled sobs and prove he was man enough not to cry, at least. She was useful, she saw then, and hated him as fiercely as she loved him for his part in the sham of walled protection, entrapping them both, and her own soft melting part in it, as practiced and as hateful and lovely as the flowers at her feet—some of them hers, cut off in full bloom. All their flowers broke open in colors more sorrowful than human eyes can swallow alone.

It was then her heavy-headed snuffling shifted its shape. Something toothed in her, large and shambling on warm thigh muscle, stood up inside, ferocious and whole.

THEY SHOUT PRAISES

Raoul wakes up believing that Virney is still there. The sunlight coming in the east window is just-washed, smelling of summer rain, and he forgets until he stretches out an arm that she isn't under the sheets next to him.

He has an old Graflex set up on a tripod next to the window. It's the first thing he sees every morning. For six months he's taken the same picture of the same elm tree in the side yard, every day, the same picture, same ancient technology, but different weather, different light, sometimes a person in the frame, or an object.

And when he first sees that shaft of hazy light, slanting in like some message from God, he thinks, Virney, look at this, what a shot this'll make with the aperture wide open.

He feels smooth, flat surface next to him, remembers their last fight, and recalls now that it has gone on all night in several convoluted versions without missing a beat. He can almost see her there, bunching the sheets up on top of her chest as she sits up to leave, her straw-textured hair wild, and her blue eyes pale ice. She says: "You really think it's all about f-stops and apertures, don't you?"

He made a show of it, the first few days after she left, getting out of bed and taking that picture of the elm just as if nothing had happened. He wanted a full year's diary; he could see it in his mind.

But she ruined it. He missed yesterday. Today he can't get up. He stays in bed until the sun is straight overhead, the moisture burned out of the light, until it is hot and clear, and the shadows outside are sharp-edged.

He lies there for so long he starts imagining he can feel his own beard growing, pictures his body wasting away, thinks how she will feel when they find him here, ruined, alone, goddammit.

A good thing, a good thing he has an assignment, he stops himself, looking at the clock. The Pilgrim Rest Tabernacle. That ought to be a challenge.

He believes that his work, his art, is good for the soul. It's what Virney always said. It's what they had in common; they were going to be artists: he, the photographer, and she, welding hubcaps and copper brushes to old bathroom fixtures and buckets, sculptures that nobody but the two of thBy now he has taken photos at just about every church in town, but this is his first wedding at Pilgrim Rest just past the strip of fast food restaurants outside town. Overnight this church popped up like a mushroom. They delivered it in two pieces on a flatbed truck, and then snapped it together on top with a steeple that looked as if it were part of some kid's plastic block set.

Raoul often drives past the church. He likes watching it. The church folks have put cement blocks up to the door for steps and a handmade wooden sign near the door that says: "Sunday School, Sunday morning services, Sunday evening services and Wednesday night prayer meeting. 'Come unto me, and I will give thee rest.'" It sounded to him like a lot of work, going to church that many times a week.

They never mowed their lawn, though, which makes Raoul think they might have a few right ideas. He never mows his lawn either. It makes his neighbors stay away from him, that and his long, dark hair and the name, Raoul Comstock, which sounds as weird as he wants it to. His real name is Francis, or as his family calls him, Frank.

Frank had met Virney, then Virginia, at Western U. and they'd escaped from Kalamazoo to find Rutland and an old Vermont house unpainted for so long it was down to the natural wood. Virney liked that. For long enough to save for a darkroom for him and a workshop for her, they got by on some money Frank had in trust from his grandmother for when he graduated from college. Which he finally had at twenty-seven.

God, they froze that first winter, stuffing wood into a potbelly stove as fast as the heat leaked out the cracks. They finally hung blankets on clotheslines like a teepee in a square inside the front room where the stove was, and lived in that space, put a mattress on the floor, cooked soup and coffee on the stove top. Meanwhile, the kitchen pipes froze solid. The only reason the john didn't freeze was because it was broken and running constantly. It was like going outside. Whoever sat first on the icecold seat would bellow for the entertainment of the other; Virney could out-bellow Frank any day.

Finally, they had to have more money. That summer Virney looked for a job at a metal shop, but had to settle for an aide's job at a nursing home. Jobs in Vermont were a pisser, Ph.Ds working as waitresses. And when she started getting bitchy about her forty hours, he broke down and had some business cards made to offer his services as a wedding photographer.

Frank half meant it as a joke. Another reason for the name Raoul. He left them at drug stores and at dress shops where they rented tuxes and sold wedding dresses. He put the cards up on grocery store bulletin boards. He started getting calls. Lots of calls. He had thought marriage was on the way out, but not in Rutland, Vermont, it wasn't. And neither were churches.

Raoul doesn't know much about theology, or what the popped-up Tabernacle people believe that is so different from the New Testament Faith Evangelical church in town. Except that they speak in tongues and yell when the Spirit moves them. One time they were shouting so loud that he and Virney, driving past, could hear them, and she told him how a great aunt of hers had dragged her to a Pentecost church one time.

"That's how they do it," she said. "They shout praises."

Since Virney left, Raoul has relished the idea that she'd be jealous of Susan Ribb. Susan Ribb happens to be the bride in the Pilgrim Rest wedding and also the worst flirt Raoul has ever come across. If he hadn't known the girl was a Bible believer, he would have guessed she was a little sexpot.

When she came for her portrait session, he explained how the silver umbrella, upside down on the floor, bounced light on her face and would make her look twice as good. She said, yes, she wanted to look good all right, so she could look back on this time and remember how young she was to be buried alive.

He said, "Excuse me?"

She said he'd heard her right. Marriage for her was like being buried alive. No more parties, no more drinking. And he said, "Wait a minute. I thought you were getting married at the Pilgrim Rest. Aren't they all teetotalers?"

She said, yes, her father was a minister, and he was going to be mighty relieved to have her married because she had been so wild, and they wanted her to start in having babies right away because they knew that would settle her down.

Then she said, "They don't care much for the man I picked." The look on her face said she thought she's outsmarted somebody and gotten revenge. Her fiancé's name was Lucky Harrison.

She was in the middle of explaining this while Raoul straightened her veil and lifted her chin a little for the next shot. He noted her long blonde hair, her plump little cheeks, full pouty lips—Christ! Every cell in that girl's body looked turgid with juice—and she was looking up at him with eyes that were—oh, he knew he wasn't seeing things—inviting.

He protected himself with a question about her man. "So what's with Lucky that your parents don't approve?"

"Oh, Lucky talks a big show, but he's really all right. Daddy thinks he's a hood because he has a motorcycle and wears a leather jacket sometimes. But he's never been in trouble with the law or anything. He's been trying real hard to please my daddy, just so he can marry me. Which is why we're getting married in church. I would have run off with him."

"You would?" Raoul asked. "Why?"

"Because it'd be something different. I don't want to do what everybody else is doing."

"Well, why are you getting married then?"

He could see from her expression that she didn't have a good answer for this and it bothered her.

Virney would have jumped right in and tried to talk her out of it then and there. "Marriage won't solve anything," she'd have said.

"You know," Raoul said. Maybe you shouldn't rush into anything."

A light came on in Susan's head: The Wrong Idea. She smiled slowly, tilted her head. "Why? Does it bother you, my getting married?"

She came and stood close to him, real close, and Raoul didn't know what to do. Nothing like this had ever happened before, so he just stood there. She put her arms around his neck, crisp lace and taffeta rustling from the movement.

He said, "What would Lucky think? Seeing us like this?"

And she said, "I'm not Mrs. Harrison. Yet."

"I got a feeling you like to shock people, is that right?"

She lowered her arms, stared at him a moment, mad that he hadn't just melted. "You're cute," she said. "But you don't have much nerve."

⁂

Since then Raoul has ventured into more and more outrageous sexual fantasies about Susan Ribb, the one reprieve he has from Virney in his dreams. Since Susan is not your average bride, he goes to the wedding with plenty of extra film for himself, still enough of an artist to indulge in extra shots if he is inspired. Susan wants Deluxe Wedding Package A, which means Raoul can circulate and get lots of candids.

He takes some early shots of The Reverend Ribb greeting guests at the door. The Reverend's shoulders are held back in an exaggeratedly upright posture, his chest barrel-like, accounting for his resonant voice. The man has all his hair, swept back in a plume from his forehead like Raoul, but his glance makes it clear that he doesn't approve of the way Raoul's locks continue on behind his ears and down to his shoulders. A parched-looking Mrs. Ribb is tucked in behind one of her husband's shoulders, mirroring his expressions.

Raoul puts his extra equipment and tripod in a pew near the back, and then sets off to find Susan. Downstairs in a classroom with her maid of honor, she is seated on a desk top, her feet dangling above the floor, decked in white pumps and white stockings and the wedding dress Raoul remembers; he has plagued himself with visions of lifting the skirt.

White netting spouts from a beaded crown on top of her head. Susan looks down, being still enough so that the other girl, who has on a large picture hat, can draw a deep blue line next to her lashes. When they hear the shutter click, they both look up.

"Raoul Comstock," Susan says, hopping down and picking up her bouquet from another desk top. She keeps on smiling after he smiles in greeting, smiling and staring.

"Just go on with what you were doing, Miss Ribb," he says. "These'll turn out better if you just pretend I'm not even here."

"It's hard to pretend you're not here," she says. She and her friend both enjoy seeing him squirm. They put their heads together and giggle, and the maid of honor goes to a bag and pulls out a pint of whiskey. They both take a swig, as if to dare Raoul to get that on film.

He does. They all laugh, and he shares a swig with them, but then he says, "I'd better go find the groom."

⁓

Lucky is out near the road with a group of young men dressed in black suits with satin stripes down the sides of the pants. He is distinguished by a rose-colored shirt, the same color as the maid of honor's dress.

Raoul introduces himself, but Lucky isn't listening. He looks pale and keeps staring out toward the road while he smokes a cigarette. When Raoul asks to bum one, he reaches inside his satin jacket, still gazing the other way.

"You better not let the Reverend see you out here with Demon Nicotine," a younger brother kids him. "He would put a halt to this whole thing, I'll bet. He would lock Miss Susan right up. What if they wouldn't let you go through with this? What would you do? Celebrate?" The young men laugh uproariously, without pity for the groom.

"It's natural being nervous about this," Lucky says, putting his hand down next to his pant leg to hide his cigarette. "Wait until you get married."

The ceremony is short, the only long part being the sermon by the Reverend Ribb, full of admonitions about the state of marriage today, and people who don't even bother anymore because they know they'll just get divorced, and what is everything come to with families split apart more than they're kept together?

Raoul begins thinking about his last fight with Virney,

how she'd taken him out to the workshop to surprise him—
their two-year anniversary—with a ring she'd made out of
two brass pipe fittings. On the spot, he'd guiltily decided to
leave the new bulk loader he just bought with his last thirty
bucks out in the car for the time being.

Now he sees clearly that he should have just put on
the ring, thanked her kindly, and let it go at that. But he was
embarrassed at forgetting their day and maybe he wanted to
outdo her, so he proposed.

She looked as if he'd slapped her in the face.

He sits there in the church pew, thinking, maybe it was
the way he did it. Like he didn't really mean it. Did he mean it?

"Oh, just like that. I'll be the mommy and you be the daddy.
Like some of those pictures you take, all neat and framed."

"No, honest, I think we should—"

"I've already told you. I'm not marrying anyone ever again."

"Okay." He shrugged.

"I want something more than that, Frank. I want...."
She gestured furiously. "I want connection. Intimacy."

"Okay."

She glared at him. "Do you know? You are like
mercury; I can't hold you."

"I'm here. Hold me, go ahead."

"I mean you. You. You won't let me close. You want to
marry me so you can keep me at a safe distance. The form,
not the substance. The technicalities, not the—the soul." She
pounded her sternum until it made a thumping noise.

He sits in the church pew and still doesn't know what
she was talking about. Wasn't that what he was offering
her? What did marriage mean if it didn't mean commitment,
closeness? What would be so bad about marrying him?

Another time he remembers: holding Virney in the kitchen. Dozens of strips of film were clipped like wash to a string he'd stretched across the ceiling.

Her head was on his shoulder. She was crying because, she said, she was too tired. How could she ever finish that sculpture? What hope did she have it would turn out right, the way that she felt it, she could feel it—God, the frustration!

And he looked out over her head to study the negative right behind her. 27A looks pretty good, he thought, stretching his neck to see better. He should have framed the shot though, another f-stop either way might have....

She must have felt it in his touch, looked up to catch him craning and squinting. He pretended to have a crick in his neck. She said, "Bastard. You weren't even listening...."

❧

Now comes the part of the ceremony where the lights are dimmed, the bride and groom, given lighted tapers. Both light a third candle on a small table in front of the altar and blow out their own.

A symbol, Reverend Ribb intones, of the sanctity of marriage: where once there were two, now there is only this God-sanctioned one. Always, Raoul remembers, there is a moment like this in the marriage ceremony, and always, Virney would lean over and whisper, "Yeah, but which one will they be?"

Afterwards there are family portraits, noteworthy because of the enormous size of Lucky's mother compared to the size of his father, as if he'd been cannibalized. Seeing them coupled with Reverend Ribb and his worn out wife, Raoul wonders about Virney's theory of marriage; maybe she is right, but he decides the Ribb wedding still has its moments. There are real faces here, folks who didn't have it easy.

And Susan is pretty; Lucky looks like he feels lucky. Raoul sees that, at least when Susan is with Lucky, she wants to do the right thing and love him.

Raoul takes more photos than usual. The light in the basement, where the reception happens, is terrible, but he likes the drama it adds.

"How come you wear long hair?" a boy asks him. The kid has on a suit and tie and his hair is patent leather slick. "Are you a hippy?"

"I was once. Now I can't afford it."

The kid eyes his equipment. Raoul says: "This stuff cost me a quarter of a million dollars. You touch it, I'll have you arrested." The kid backs off and in a few minutes, Raoul sees him taking his frustration out on another kid under the wedding cake table. That makes for a few good shots.

Mostly people ignore him. He gets shots of people with their heads together talking, pictures of young girls who aren't used to their high heels and stockings yet. The old folks are grim, or they are cheery, their lined faces the maps of long distant places.

Lucky and Susan bring him a slice of cake and some small talk. Lucky has his arm around her and she suddenly looks shy, maybe afraid Raoul will give her away.

"We'll be opening our gifts next," she says, and he nods, a fork still lodged in his mouth, patting his camera at his side to show he is ready.

Then she asks, "Is there a Mrs. Comstock? Or have all these weddings turned you off?"

"No, there isn't. But it's not the weddings. The weddings make me sentimental. It's my girl—Virginia—who's the problem."

"Won't tie the knot, huh?" Lucky laughs and tightens his armlock on Susan.

"She got burned once."

"Does she love you?"

Raoul thinks about that. "Yes."

Susan shrugs, as if to say, so what's the problem? "Do you love her?"

When he hesitates, a lusty light comes on in her eyes, The Wrong Idea again, a knee-jerk urge to prove her power, the only power she knows she has so far. She glances at Lucky to see if he's noticed and is jealous.

Raoul can see the two of them will have a time of it. So damned young and unsure of themselves. Married for lack of imagination.

Poor Lucky has all he can do to keep his hands off her, though, and Susan, she eggs him on. Watching her move through the lens, Raoul gets hot just thinking about later. Virney would say it was tyranny, the boxes young people get put into, just so they can slake a simple thirst.

Just then the Reverend walks past with his wife, who looks as if she hasn't slaked any thirsts in quite a while. The Reverend is keeping an eye on Susan, not approving of her gaiety, sniffing for liquor, somehow expecting her to be more matronly now. Susan's sins, objectionable enough when single, now weigh heavier; Raoul captures it in his camera.

He gets a few shots of people praying together, their hands above their heads, their lips moving rapidly. "What are they doing?" he asks Lucky who is nearby, watching them, too.

"They're praising God," he says. "Speaking in tongues." He looks at Raoul as if to say he doesn't understand it either, but hey, these are his folks now.

Raoul can make out a babble of syllables, interspersed with, "Praise you, Jesus, praise God, alleluia," a racket like the time he and Virney drove past.

He drinks a lot that night at home, and does it alone, unusual for him. It is late morning by the time he wakes up, remembering a long dream that intertwined and mystified and still seems to lie ahead of him somehow. There'd been sex and Susan and more bodies than that, and Virney was there with her face uplifted, her hands above her head. She was speaking in tongues. She had got religion.

Raoul gets up to look through the lens of the Graflex, exposes a frame automatically, and has breakfast, thinking about the afternoon ahead of him in the darkroom. That will be fine.

Then supper, the evening looming ahead, a broad, empty highway headed for the horizon, no houses on either side. He shakes his head. More snatches of dream.

He thinks: God, I miss Virney. That's the truth.

She told him when she left, "When you figure out what you want, you call me."

When I figure out what I want. What the hell does that have to do with anything? I never wanted to be a wedding photographer. I never wanted to be alone.

"I wanted you," he hears her answer. "That's different from not wanting to be alone. Look at me. Tell me I wasn't just convenient."

Well, she was convenient. She came along at just the right time; it seemed to fit. What was wrong with that?

Raoul takes the first contact sheet out of the fixer, and right away he sees how good his eye is. Virney would have seen it. "Virney," Raoul lectures, "the secret of a good artist's eye is distance. You get too close to a subject, you start forming opinions, wanting certain things too much, and it won't turn out. You can't get too close."

"Horseshit," she ups the ante. "I am the steel when I'm working it." And he clips the last sheet, with its negatives, breathing a laugh, thinking, Jesus, watch out: Virney with her blowtorch.

He's after a particular photo of Susan, looking completely unsuited to her costume, which is what he likes about it. He flicks on the safe-light, dodges and burns, until he has the print just right.

This one's of Lucky with his arm around Susan, checking out a toaster oven, Lucky saying how he always liked three pieces of toast every morning and Raoul's shutter, catching him expounding on how it ought to be, while Susan looked the other way.

Lucky, Raoul salutes him, plunging the print under running water, good luck. She's not into toast, I can tell you, and maybe you're luckier than you know.

Virney melted a toaster into a fountain part once, a shiny ledge that spread the water into a thin, even sheet. He set up his umbrella to show her how lighting can add drama, and the falling water gleamed so brilliantly they both laughed, embarrassed to be that delighted.

The afternoon is gone before he realizes it. He thinks how it always happens this way. He loves the images, the shades of light and dark, the contrasts, all of it. Maybe he was the film, the way Virney said she was the steel when she made it happen.

He thinks: I could call her.

"Call me when you know what you want," she'd said.

Another print. People with hands overhead, some of them with eyes closed, all intent. They call it religious ecstasy.

Virney said art was that way. Art made time irrelevant—and with her sex was like that, too. He thinks of a series of nude photos he took of parts of her—the shadows of hollows, the lights of curves. "I don't recognize myself," she said when he showed them to her. "Oh, they're you," he breathed against her neck.

"Look at me," she'd said then, pushing him back. "This is me." She'd been out in the garage, welding. She had on her mechanic's jumpsuit, one piece that zippered. Okay, he thought, here comes the holistic artist statement, integrity and all that blah blah.

She unzipped then, and let the single piece of clothing fall to the floor. She had nothing on underneath.

Raoul closes his eyes a moment. He never told her what it meant to him, seeing her offer herself like that. Shit, it comes to him now: I didn't tell myself.

"Look at me, Frank," she said, pressing herself against him. He remembers how he couldn't keep quiet that time, and Virney, she never could—and he suddenly thinks how God must hear that too, must feel praised by the tongues of lovers, and he wants to shout alleluia.

Alleluia, he could call her.

IN A HOUSE BY THE RIVER

er mother said she was sorry things weren't going well and offered to come out and stay with her awhile, but Virginia said no, she was fine really. And afterward she kept thinking it was odd the way she felt: things weren't going well, things were going very well. She was sorting the pieces out; nothing matched. She was giddy to be rid of him; she missed him.

That summer was so hot the air hung in sheets that shimmered over the streets, and in back of the Mosely's house, the grasses were prostrate. Grown tall, they fell down the slope in straw-brown rapids to the river at the bottom of the shallow ravine where she liked to walk along the river's bank. She pictured herself as she must have looked—a solitary figure with hands clasped behind her back, head down, cicadas whirring out in front of her steps like the bow wake of some magical ship.

It was a time for staring and introspection, usually there by the river. Other times, she would stand on the redwood deck off her living room and look at the lawns up Terrace Street, green even in this heat and stretched out like a single carpet. This was a good neighborhood and North Haven river property was hard to come by. Still, no one spoke to her about the way she had let the back lawn go, with the grasses tumbling toward the St. Regis.

By this time her neighbors must have surmised that

she had been abandoned. Robert Mosely's car hadn't pulled into the drive since that time two months ago when he'd backed out with the station wagon loaded with papers, a file cabinet crammed into the back, a lamp sticking out of one window.

She pictured this scene, too, so often it was like a favorite movie: his face determined, set hard against the possibility of her tears, while she is round-eyed and blinking. She has on a jogging suit, her hair that needs shampooing is twisted into a bun, and his parting words, accompanied by gestures that scorn the way she has let herself go, are: "This is the sort of thing I mean, Virginia—Look at you."

Well, the sweat pants were comfortable and she always meant to start jogging someday. And now that the weather was hot, she wore jogging shorts that she knew wouldn't have pleased him either. Just to prove some point she stopped shaving her legs too, heard his comment in her head: When did you become Italian?—and ran her hand along her shin to feel the bristles.

Those moments that were nicest, when she felt giddy from the freedom, were the ones when she suddenly realized that without thinking about it she had been doing what she wanted: she had cooked an omelet with onions, had turned the television off after the news, had decided to go for a walk in the dark and been completely silent. There was peace in this self-centeredness and it pleased her very much and worried her.

Other times she missed Robert. Or missed someone. If it hadn't been for Rheba the Avon lady she would have been completely alone the past two months. God! she heard Robert say in her head. This was just the sort of thing he was talking about. Making up to that woman instead of to the Rumfords next door. Or the Maxwells, what was wrong with them? Not colorful enough to suit her? After a while he'd begun referring to Rheba as your friend the dancing bear.

She'd been fascinated with Rheba from the time she first appeared at the front door. Something about her reminded her of a woman from her childhood, a Mrs. Murphy at whose house she'd stayed when just a little girl and her mother was struggling to survive after her divorce. Her memories of Mrs. Murphy were of being bundled in a blanket in a rocker next to the coal stove, country music, blaring in the background, and twangy conversations going on in the kitchen while she was supposed to be asleep.

She invited Rheba in, though she had never bought anything from the other Avon ladies who visited, or even looked at a catalog before. The woman tread lightly on the carpet, respectful of her surroundings, though not overly so. "You could cook a whole hawg in there," was her comment as she passed the fieldstone fireplace that divided the living room from the dining room. And when she noticed the hearth was open, she bent down to peer through. Where on earth had she come from? The hills of Kentuck?

No, years ago from Tennessee, it turned out; only now she lived seven miles up Gold Star Highway in a run-down place that Virginia had noticed before—leaning slightly, unpainted, with lumpy hillocks of grass in the front and a hand-painted sign that advertised live bait and underneath that another that said: "Collie Pups 4 Sale. Rabbits Live and Dressed." This wasn't Rheba's usual territory she explained. But the regular girl was out pregnant and she'd offered to fill in. She needed the money for seed corn.

If Avon had been looking, they couldn't have found a less likely candidate for selling beauty products. She pulled her coarse hair back into a pony tail that was more like that of a draft horse, while her face, shiny and scrubbed, was make-up free. She was perhaps 15 years older than Virginia, about 50, she guessed, though it was hard to tell because of the way she didn't fit into the usual categories. She had on a mint green pantsuit that would have appalled Robert if he'd been there that afternoon, and oxford shoes on her feet that might have been a man's.

Every page they turned brought a comment from Rheba, and the amazing thing was how sincere they were: "Ain't this a pretty thing," she said about the hand-lotion dispenser shaped like a cob of corn. And "Lookit this purple stuff she puts around her eye. Looks good on her though."

Since that first time she had learned that on Saturdays and Sundays Rheba put up a stand at the Frobisch Flea Market up the Gold Star Highway from her: her collection of Avon bottles had to be set up six rows deep. "I got people come from three states away, all the way from Wisconsin to see my bottles," she told Virginia, "and they buy'em too. But some I won't sell."

Maybe it was Rheba's sincerity, more likely it was just her desire to have the woman come back, but Virginia ordered toothpaste on special and the "Love is a Rainbow" decorator plate. As a matter of fact, Robert was there the afternoon Rheba delivered it, had in fact just ended a discussion he'd insisted on having with the suggestion that she see a lawyer. As she recalled it now, she had answered that she wasn't the one who wanted a divorce after all, and the doorbell had rung.

If Rheba had been the sort to pick up on body language and bad vibrations, she might have had the good sense to come back later. Virginia imagined the place rocking from the vibrations right then, lamps tipping, pictures on the wall awry—but once inside, Rheba had only asked for directions to the little girl's room, nodded at Robert on her way and then called out, "Be right back you two. Won't take me long to water the garden."

"Who the hell was that?" Robert said.

"She's a wonderful person—one of a kind."

"Oh yes. I can see that. I'll just bet they broke the mold after that one," he said and stormed off to the bedroom.

In retrospect, Virginia wondered if it hadn't been the "Love Is a Rainbow" plate that was the final straw for them. She had hung it over the bed and when Robert was shocked at her bad taste, she had answered that somehow it struck her as appropriate.

Three months after Rheba came into her life, Robert had left. Somewhere in there Rheba became her friend, or at least had become a central occasion. Rheba's friendliness was a constant, rather than particular, Virginia suspected, like a good-natured retriever who kept coming back because Virginia kept buying things, even things she didn't need: red nail polish she wouldn't be caught dead in, bath oil though she only showered, a heavy metal necklace she fantasized giving to Robert for Christmas just to show how she despised him, and, she thought with a sinking feeling, how she kept on thinking of him in spite of herself.

"I'm going to have to get a job," she told Rheba one afternoon that she'd talked her into staying for dinner.

"Robert's lawyer says Robert will pay the mortgage until the settlement happens, but I've got the utilities and groceries and my savings are about gone."

"Well," said Rheba, "Could be as how you could get by just selling some things. I could help you set up at the flea market. Be fun to have you the next table over."

This pleased Virginia more than she could say. It was the first she'd been sure that she was more than just a customer to Rheba, and it was an idea with a certain genius. The promise of getting rid of some things appealed to her, not just because of the money it would bring. She looked around the room at the brass sconces on the wall which had been Robert's idea of a gift to her, and next thought of the vacuum cleaner—another gift. "Yes," she said to Rheba. "I could do that, couldn't I?"

By the time things had progressed enough that a settlement conference had been arranged with the four of them to be present—Virginia, Virginia's lawyer, Robert's lawyer and Robert—the house on Terrace Street was cleared of everything but the biggest pieces of furniture. It had a monastic feeling that appealed to Virginia very much, and she was aware that when she pictured the look on Robert's face when he discovered it, she felt real pleasure. In fact, as she looked back on those weeks it seemed to her that the pieces of her life were beginning to match, or if they didn't match, then at least she was discarding those that wouldn't fit any longer.

At dusk, when the heat was bearable, she took long walks that always ended at the river's bank, and after dark she made her way back up to the house by a path she'd worn through the grasses. At times she felt like a child again, with no need to do what she didn't want to do, eating only when hungry, going nowhere except where she chose to, and she chose to go nowhere except the corner market when needed, or sometimes to Rheba's to feed the rabbits and the goldfish in a sad home-made pond.

The weekend before the Tuesday meeting, she took the last few boxes of books and some dishes, and with difficulty loaded up the lawn mower, and headed for the Frobisch Flea Market. Sitting on a lawn chair next to Rheba under the shade of their own reserved maple tree, the two of them sitting behind their tables and watching people drift by—it was good, she thought.

She felt settled and safe with the drone of the crowd there, and a soft summer breeze, and then Rheba told her some developers had been by and offered her more for her property than she could earn in twenty good summers if she planted it all to corn. She was thinking of moving back to Tennessee to be close to her sister. She had been alone a good, long while. Since both her daughters had grown up.

"You can't be serious!" said Virginia. "What will I do without you? I thought we were friends!"

"So we are."

"But what will I do with you down in Tennessee?"

"Shoot, you are close to doing all kinds of things, girl. You been gathering yourself up this summer, picking up some little bit here, some chunk over there—It's so," Rheba went on, "You know you ain't gonna just sit in that house the rest of your life. Ain't I right?"

In truth, Virginia's fantasies had turned to places she had never been and given up on: San Francisco, Vermont, places hilly and scenic. And to smaller dreams:

The Department of Library Science at Western Michigan, maybe, a continuing ed course in macro-economics—Virginia didn't know what to say, scratched her hand, then bent over to scratch her sandaled foot.

"You know what that means," said Rheba. "Scratch your left hand, a stranger's coming. Scratch your right hand, and money's on its way. Scratch your right foot and you're off on a journey."

"Which hand did I just scratch?"

"Both," said Rheba. "And now you got me started," she said scratching her hand. "See? Money. More money than 20 years of good crops."

⮾

They were civilized through gritted teeth at the meeting, seated at either end of a very long table. It was crushing to discover that he looked as handsome as ever. When he turned his head, the light highlighted the angles of his face in such a familiar way, she felt pulled by some inner whirlpool; she was relieved when he spoke because of the way his tone shattered any illusions.

She was angry with him. It occurred to her now that she had been angry with him for a very long time, long before he began talking about divorce. She'd heard once that couples on the rocks did one of two things to keep from falling apart: they had babies or they built new houses. She had never wanted that house.

"My client is prepared to buy out her share in the house. He had thought he was doing the right thing by leaving her with it, but the neighbors have expressed some concern about its maintenance and her stability—and, our hope is there won't be an unnecessary battle."

"Virginia?" her lawyer turned to her and whispered. "Is this something new?"

"I told you I haven't spoken to him about it since he left. Let him have the house. Let him have everything. I'm unstable, you heard him say it."

"Unstable or crazy? You're just going to let him have it?"

"He said he'd buy me out. I'd rather have the money. I've got plans after this. That house was always his idea."

He was smarmy after the hearing, believing as he did that he had gotten away with something, which he had. "I'm glad we could settle this like adults," he said. "I must say I'm glad to see you looking so well after what the Maxwells said about your wandering around; you've had them worried. Now the rest is just technicalities. This is really better for both of us, Virginia. It was too much for you to handle anyway, from the looks of the place."

"I could handle it," she said. "I just didn't want to."

"What are your plans?" he asked, lighting up a cigarette and looking out past her shoulder.

"I'm joining a traveling circus," she said.

"What?"

"I said I'm selling wares at a flea market," she said.

"You're kidding!"

"Of course. I'm going to school. Library Science. San Francisco maybe."

"Well, good luck. I mean it. You've been restless a good long while. Me, I just want to settle down." He exhaled a stream of smoke, laughed a breathy laugh. "I'm thinking about getting married again."

This hit her hard as a fist in the stomach, and she had all she could do to hide it. "Well. That's good. You wanted to be settled. Get settled. That's right. Someone who'll make friends with the Maxwell's next door."

"Exactly," he said with a voice not completely free of malice.

It was good, she decided, that she had been forced to make that up about going to school and San Francisco. Rather like telling people you are going on a diet, and then having to start one to prove you could do it. She visited the library and learned that there were plenty of schools with majors in library science in San Francisco, and there were hills, too, just as she'd imagined it. She would have the money, she only needed to apply and then go, but she didn't write them.

"When the time comes," said Rheba, "you will know it. Don't worry yourself."

"But what if I don't really want to be a librarian. I thought I wanted to be Robert's wifey and that turned out to be wrong."

"Well, count yourself lucky you found out in due time. By the time some discover they took a wrong fork in the river, they're too tired to keep on swimming. Look at me. I'm about to take a new fork. Do you think there's no dangers? What will I do with all this?" Rheba pointed to the piles of newspapers and magazines that were stacked in every corner of the room.

The two of them were sitting in Rheba's living room,

on the only piece of furniture cleared of junk—a rose-colored lumpish sofa. "Who will take all my rabbits? Who'll clean out the pond? How do I know this is the right thing to do? Soon there will be streets of fine houses all along my strip of river, and who here will love it like I do?"

"I loved it. I still love it."

"Yes, that's right. But soon you'll be leaving it too. And you listen, girl, you will be fine. You will get past this, and both of us will be fine."

Rheba and she sorted through her Avon collection that evening, putting in boxes what Rheba thought she could sell, and in one single box those decanters that were too dear to her to part with. One of these was a gaudy painted rainbow trout, up on end on the crest of a glass wave, filled with spicey after-shave, the cap topped with a feathered fly.

"They's not many of these around," said Rheba, and then she handed it to Virginia. "You have this, from me. Go on, take it, it's worth somethin'. And you get an urge for that fella who run off for his little wootzie, you just take you a whiff a this. But you get on with your life, you hear me?"

❧

Her mother called later that week and said she was shocked to hear what Robert had done, and could she come out and stay with her awhile, but Virginia said no, she was fine, really. She had plans to go to school, and her mother said that was nice, but then what would she do? Virginia answered she didn't know. Did she have to know at this point? And her mother said, well, she wasn't getting

any younger. Mistakes at her age might not be so easy
to undo.

⁓

That afternoon, when she was cleaning up the
last bit of her belongings, she accidentally knocked over
Rheba's decanter, smashing it. The house reeked so badly of
aftershave that it gave her a headache and after cleaning up
the glass she went outside and sat on the bank of the river. It
seemed the worst possible omen, a portent of things to come.
And then as if to prove it, she heard Robert call her name,
and looking back over her shoulder she saw him standing on
the deck off the living room, some young thing next to him,
looking hopeful.

She supposed she should be mature and go up to the
house to welcome the happy couple. Instead she crowded
down closer to the river. They might have at least telephoned
to warn her, but Virginia remembered then how she'd had
the phone disconnected. Robert called her name again. She
slipped down into the water and edged over to some bushes
where she was sure she was out of sight, and waited.

To her surprise she soon heard crashing noises, as if
someone were making their way down through the grasses.
She eased farther up the shore, hanging onto the roots of the
bank, her toes digging into the soft sand underneath her. It
was ridiculous, this whole business. What if they persisted in
finding her, how would she explain it? Didn't she hear them
calling her? What was she doing swimming in her clothes in
that dirty old river?

And suddenly the whole scene seemed exactly right—

she let go of the bank and let herself be carried by the leisurely current, hidden from view by the underbrush. The thing was to keep on swimming.

Some vague plan evolved in her mind. She would swim to Rheba's place and prove she could do whatever she chose, no matter how silly it might seem to some. She would keep on swimming—four miles almost—but that was by highway, she was sure it was much less by water—a rite of passage this would be, a journey to mark her coming journey.

She watched the water flow on past her, flow on past and no retrieving it, and began to feel a part of it, protected by her own movement. She had holed herself up in that house, blamed Robert, played the eccentric, but hadn't really dared to be eccentric, except in small ways, that is, hadn't ever dared to do what she plain wanted to. What did she want to do?

Nothing monumental came to mind. Go to school maybe. Make some friends who didn't live in subdivisions. Make some friends who didn't want to do the expected things either. Well, she had one friend like that already.

She glanced back toward the big brick home with its redwood deck without any regret, and let the sound of the water around her push aside any raucous thought of what might happen. She was conscious mostly of the rhythms of her own breathing, the burning of the scratches on her bare legs, her determination to finish this journey or drown doing it. She did not really think she would drown, but she would think of this crazy time in years that came after, imagining how she might have fallen into a sink hole when she began wading in the water, but that was only salutary—her tip of the hat to what she thought others might say about it.

In fact, she thought it the sanest thing she had done that summer, lowering herself into that cool water in that heavy heat.

She waded when the river grew shallow, but most of the time she was buoyant, paddling to steer herself, letting the water rise up to her nostrils as she floated with the current. Toward the end she was nearly exhausted, which was frightening because she didn't know for sure that she was close to the end, knew only that she had come a very long way—longer than Robert would have bet on, longer than she would have bet on herself.

The sun was gathering color low in the sky and she began to think she would have to finish her journey in the dark. She began to think of what snakes there might be in the water, or horrible garfish, but the thing about it was that she had to keep on going, that was the thing she could see in the river, the simplest thing and the hardest. And she kept paddling, bumping along the bottom here and there, grabbing onto tree roots to give herself a push.

She saw a clearing she thought looked familiar. There were some lights on a hill. She stood up in the water near the bank and recognized Rheba's house from the way its barn leaned. Silhouetted against a pink and golden sky, Rheba was in the garden in back of the barn, still a distance from the lowlands. She straightened now and rubbed a forearm across her face.

Virginia called out without thinking how the sight of her might startle Rheba. Climbing out of the river, half staggering, half crawling, wet hair plastered down her neck, she finally stood on the bank and waved for all she was worth. Years later, while she was driving along a flat stretch of highway at dusk, it occurred to Virginia that she was happy, and she suddenly remembered how her heart had leaped a little to see that Rheba recognized her all the way from the garden and was waving her arm back in answer in that tawny light, as if it were the most natural thing in the world to see her there by the river and welcome her.

GOLDFISH

L ast night Ann slipped back into girlhood, flopping around in waters, uncertain, way in over her head again. It always happens the moment her mother enters the picture, the reason she tries to keep her out of it—which isn't hard because her mother Margaret has always kept herself hidden. Ann had forgotten she still swims beneath her; she breathes water.

Ann remembered again last night. Her own daughter, Alex, grown up now, had called Ann about travelling on a work assignment, near enough to stop in to visit her grandmother.

"We had to take poor Toots to the vet, his wheezing got so bad. She was upset we had to leave him there overnight. That little dog's all she has anymore, and even so, late as it was, she fixed me supper," her daughter intoned—

Ann recognized the echoes in her voice. They all used guilt to describe her mother's white ruffled curtains, her kitschy knick-knacks and their own hectic schedules. Alone now, Ann's mother Margaret mostly waited without hope, most family dead now, or moved off to distant places—and even so, in the middle of her crisis—"Exhausted as she was," Alex told her, "Gram baked me cookies to take home."

Ann couldn't stop herself. "What kind?" she asked.

"Oatmeal," Alex answered, biting golden lace before she breathed, "with raisins."

They paid a moment of silence obeisance. They both knew that Ann had never matched her mother's oatmeal cookies, or her self-sacrifice, while Alex had never attempted either. Alex dressed in business suits and ate in restaurants or out of the microwave; she focused on her brilliant career, no crime for her. Neither alluded to the bad blood between Ann and her mother because there was nothing new in this and, besides, it didn't apply.

Somehow Margaret had gotten older and kinder and was now impersonating someone tolerant of a woman's ambitions in a way she had never been of Ann's. Margaret approved of Alex, her unmarried granddaughter, who now talked as if grandma were some friendly stranger who didn't know all that much about Ann—the last part true enough, Ann thought meanly.

Alex said goodbye, and the quiet of Ann's apartment swelled and swashed. Light sank into twilight and she felt herself falling into a muddied rabbit hole, on her way down, having fallen for the oatmeal cookie that said, "Eat me." She grew smaller by the moment, small enough to enter a drop of water that fell on the floating table next to her, encountering the mother she had known and remembered, the one who had not even asked Alex about her.

The water must have come from her mother's sprinkling bottle, because there Margaret stands, dampening shirts and dresses with a stoppered Coke bottle, the glass kind you never see anymore. She rolls and stacks clothes like cordwood on the wide end of her pine ironing board, while Ann plays on the floor by her feet. Her mother presses with certainty, keeps on bearing down despite wooden groans, making of the creaking a rhythm: plunk and hiss of her iron.

Scorched damp fills the room, and her mother looks out over Ann's head and does not see her—not here—not even then.

Oh, you might think, an epiphany, and so early in the story, but this is only diving to boggy bottom, to where Ann remains her mother's child. She is living with Margaret and her new stepfather in a brown-shingled house on Niles Avenue, at the oldest edge of a new development. It has a coal furnace down in the basement, and her mother's new washing machine is down there too, the just-invented kind without a wringer. There are sidewalks in the neighborhood, which end at the street that separates their place from the newer ranch houses headed toward town, eight to a block, varied with pastel colors.

Their house, a bungalow, marks the way back to orchards and open fields. It has a row of pear trees out front where a sidewalk ought to be, and their driveway isn't smooth cement. Brown puddles form in ruts of blue-blackened cinders that her stepfather disposes of on the driveway. Ann loves to wade in these but isn't allowed; the polio vaccine hasn't yet been invented.

To the south of them, the Odet's farmhouse sits back off the road, looking like an odd duck out in the middle of a big, grassy pond. The Odets don't have a garage but a big barn and some outbuildings. Across the street, their vineyards grow untended—what with Mrs. Odet, a widow now and, some people say, a little crazy, letting things go.

Ann's stepfather has taken her bow hunting for pheasant in the tall grass of the vineyard. They never saw one, but Ann knows what pheasant look like because they're inside her house. They take flight on the living room wallpaper her mother has chosen for its drama, the brown and green birds flashing crimson wattles that match their new living room set. The field of their carpet is the green of a St. Patrick's Day parade, but red furniture springs up from it, bright and plump as dangerous mushrooms.

Ann tries not to catch the buckles of her shoes on the furniture's loopy fabric. Her mother likes to keep things nice. When they first saw the matched set in the showroom at Monkey Wards, her mother had asked her if she liked it, but forgot to listen for the answer, studying the couch as she held out her hand to demand Ann's too-big wad of bubblegum.

Ann had wanted to tell her that, most of all, she loves the fringe made of satiny cord, twisted together. She loves unraveling it because, as soon as she lets go, it twists back together again. No one knows that she does this. No one knows much of what she does here that matters to her.

Her mother is busy planting wallpaper gardens. In the kitchen where she irons, ivy climbs up a white trellis from the wainscoting, stopping at the windowed breakfast nook. They eat their meals, seated on the red, chubby cushions of a booth, surrounded by white net priscillas. Her mother bleaches these and dries them on special racks, spearing the edges on metal needles that stretch the fabric smooth and tight, everything smooth and tight in that house, clean and smelling of soap and floor wax and wallpaper paste.

Ann's room upstairs got papered last. It overlooks the backyard, which her mother insisted be fenced round with chicken wire the first year they moved here, planting vines to hide it. The St. Regis is too close nearby, its waters within sight from the Odet's barn. When Ann gets up in the mornings, she looks out her bedroom window to watch her mother, never letting her know, or she'd be sent off on some errand, or be found in need of some correction.

She studies her mother, who is bending and straightening, a clothespin between her teeth as she grabs the corners of sheets that billow. She snaps them straight, smoothing the edges before pinning them. On the fence behind her, morning glories trumpet blue.

Ann is expected to stay inside this yard, but she's nearly ten now, discontented with her sandbox and dolls. It's the summer her stepfather, Vince, gets laid off. Her mother is waiting on tables, second shift, and as soon as she backs the car out of the driveway each afternoon, Ann gives Vince a pleading look, until he nods okay, and then she heads kitty-corner across the front yard, through the small peach orchard between their house and the Odets'. As long as she's within calling distance at suppertime, Vince never misses her.

Ann ranges over fields that surround their place. Her new friend Nancy Odet shows her the secrets of their barn, the half-caved-in greenhouse, and the dump piles. During the school year Ann has never played with the Odet girl, because Jackie, the girl Ann's mother calls her best friend, thinks that Nancy's hair smells smuffy.

Jackie lives in a peach-colored ranch house in the neighborhood with sidewalks and she never falls down on her roller skates at school because she can practice every day on her cement driveway. Her clothes are pretty, and her mother does not avoid deep cleaning, according to Ann's mother, who puts great store in shiny floors free of wax buildup in the corners.

However, her mother also deplores being stuck-up, and for this reason she tolerates Ann's befriending poor Nancy whose mother, as everyone knows, is a little bit cracked, and whose older sister, Kathy, works so hard to look decent. What Ann's mother doesn't know, and what Ann and her stepfather will never tell her, is that Ann has begun to live at the Odets and ignore Jackie and her boring Barbie dolls.

Ann knows what her mother means about Mrs. Odet, though. She sells perennials as a part of her livelihood, and breeds collie dogs in kennels inside the old barn. A sign out front announces Iris and Peonies and Pups in hand-painted, red, drippy letters, while inside the circle of their drive, intended as another sort of advertisement, is a concrete goldfish pond, planted round with flowers that Mrs. Odet considers her best. Somehow she never gets around to weeding, or picking up the old flats and pots and tools that sprawl everywhere, and so, in spite of a grand scale and more grandiose vision, the overall effect celebrates disgrace.

Mrs. Odet, on those rare occasions when she decides Nancy and Ann need motherly advisement, points out a particularly hardy dahlia, or a gladiola with rare chartreuse coloring and impressive disease resistance. Next to them, hidden under lily pads that nearly cover the circle of greenish water, lolls the ocherous glint of silent, slow-moving fish.

Vince fixes late suppers of canned soup that summer, and Ann doesn't mind. Nance and she have crunched on half-ripened peaches and pears all day. They dig up small potatoes and carrots from the Odets' vegetable garden and rub them on their clothes, popping them into their mouths, ignoring grit.

Ann sneaks crusts of Kreamo bread from the breadbox, sharing bits with the fish, fascinated by the way they gulp it, soggy and green. Can they even taste what's good? She thinks twice before she throws a piece of oatmeal cookie she's found, first eating the raisins.

With so much to do, the girls rarely go inside the Odets' filthy house, much as they enjoy it. Mrs. Odet never worries about cleaning, deep or otherwise, or whether they're using coasters, or have brushed their teeth. She only wants to give them as much grape juice as they can possibly hold. She even lets them make their own secret house up in the hayloft of the barn.

They drape blankets over a clothesline and on the musty smelling floor, and it is here they center a kerosene lamp, which Mrs. Odet has not allowed. Nance has found it in the machine shop downstairs and swears her mother won't mind, transporting it up, hidden in a blanket. They light it with stolen kitchen matches. By the lantern's oily light, sitting cross-legged in woolen darkness, they eat an entire package of Jell-O, spilled out into their palms and licked until their tongues are sore.

By mid-July Ann's mother has deduced that Vince might not always know Ann's whereabouts when she's away. She complains about the amount of dirt ground into Ann's clothes, the scratches and mosquito bites on her legs. Vince says she's just upset because the layoff is going longer than it should have. He's thinking maybe he should look for another job, one at the new plastics plant.

"And lose your seniority?" Ann's mother demands. "That doesn't make sense!"

"I just don't like having any woman of mine working," Vince protests, which strikes Ann as odd, since she's never seen her mother doing anything else.

Mother turns away to dial down the front burner of the stove before the lid boils off the pot. "Beggars can't be choosers," her words fly out, their strength surprising Ann, like the fishes' had, popping out wet bread before they sucked it down again and ate it. Later in the bathroom, her mother scolds her, "I won't have you looking like some hillbilly." She scrubs Ann's back and behind her ears until they feel like they might catch on fire.

Now that she's grown, Ann can understand. Her mother had conventional dreams. She wanted to live in a house with sidewalks, wanted to own, not rent, and be a stay-at-home mom and clean the house and have the right sort of daughter inside her fence. Working for money embarrassed her; it left essentials undone. Meals still had to be planned, the shopping done, the floors kept clean, appearances maintained. Vince remained the boss, even when she thought his ideas foolish and said so. She needed him to be the boss, needed him for even brown-shingled status because without him—they would be the Odets.

Ann's mother looks up from her ironing board at that thought, catching Ann's tone, and her eyes look empty of patience as she parks the steaming iron on end. In the moistness beneath the person Ann has become, she shrinks from her mother's look that says: do you really think you know so much about me?

Ann can see her mother remembers having worked all night, having gotten up early to do the laundry, only to have to deal with naïve superiority from some smarty-pants who has gone off to college and could stand to learn a thing or two, believe you me. This is in the set of Margaret's jaw, and the way she bites off two words, the silence between them instructing her: "No. Whining!"

"I wasn't whining—"

"There you go. Right there! Did you hear yourself just then?" Satisfied, Margaret picks up the iron, and Ann shuts up, insides flipping and squirming as she listens to the hiss, watching the right-angle of her mother's elbow press down, while she adds, "Tomorrow we'll go shopping for a new school dress for you. Something pretty." She smiles at Ann's steaming jeans, now knife-creased through the patches she's ironed on.

She means that Ann's vacation is nearly over. She speaks of the awakening Ann will get once past girlhood. But wait. Is Ann remembering this right? Would her mother actually smile at her scalding demise, anticipating feminine curtailments? Did she really so look forward to Ann's sharing in female miseries?

Her mother never doubted Ann's tomboy comeuppance. She did seem gleeful in that moment, sure of Ann's coming lessons, trusting that if she couldn't teach her daughter, then the rest of the world would. How could she have anticipated Ann's whole generation of girls refusing to give themselves up? They took credit for changing the world, and feeling judged, Ann's mother grew more silent, insulted by the notion of any education and career on par with motherhood and home. She sniffed at the way Ann had cheated herself out of what was most important.

Still that didn't answer the question that most stung. Why would Ann's mother hope only for success for her Alex, and never, not ever, for her own girl, for her own daughter Ann?

A mother's love is *special,* they say. Truisms grow barbs in Ann's mouth. She feels dragged back under water.

⁓

School started after that and Ann wears her new dresses. She has to. Girls aren't allowed to wear slacks or play in the Little League, or shoot arrows, or stay out after dark. The weather grows colder, and her mother still has her waitressing job, though this worries Vince because, he says, she's in the family way now and has to keep this hidden.

Ann isn't sure what he means, but feels ashamed for her mother's sake, having to keep her family a secret. Sure it is her fault, Ann tries to be quieter.

Because frost is coming soon, Nance and her older sister and her mother drain the cement lily pond so they can capture the goldfish, who wouldn't survive winter in a shallow pond. They siphon water off, bucket by bucket, and Ann helps. In winter the basement is chock-a-block with washtubs filled with fish, cool enough down in the cellar that they stay motionless, unharmed and suspended in their lives, and here's the amazing part, Nance says—not even eating until spring when they're released again.

All summer they had floated like golden dirigibles beneath the lilies, and now in washtubs with the water low, their scales flash brass, exposed to the light; their bodies loop like rope.

"Here, fishy," Nance croons down in the Odets' basement, entered through a pair of metal doors like the hold on some great ship. The girls liked to pretend this. They stop whenever bossy Kathy is around.

Gently, gently, Nance lifts the end of a tarred bag to release the water into the washtub and finally, a fish. "We did this last year," Kathy says, seeing Ann's worry. "They like it down here in the basement. Honest." She touches the back fin to show Ann the fish's new tame nature, stunned, in the cool dark. They run back upstairs to get the rest.

It surprises Ann when her stepfather's voice calls her through the peach trees, their branches already leafless, now disappearing into dark. She runs at a lope, brushing her hands down her front, noticing for the first time that she's soaked with smelly water, black with mold and slime from the bottom of the pond.

"I thought you were in the backyard," Vince lies when he sees her. "Where were you all this time?"

"Over at the Odets. Helping put the goldfish away."

"Putting fish away—what kind of nonsense? God, look at you. Your mother's right, you have to quit all your running around the neighborhood like some wild hillbilly."

He keeps up his scolding while he runs Ann's bath water, swishing it with his hands. "She's going to kill me when she sees these clothes. Next month had better be different, young lady, once I start in on dayshift. Your mother's not going to stand for your monkey business, not with all she's got on her mind—what with a new baby on the way? You kind of excited about that? Won't it be nice, having a little baby brother to help take care of?"

Hands look like fishes underwater, she notices, and moves hers together, as if praying underwater, half-listening, half-thinking he must be crazy. What was he talking about?

Even remembering, Ann slides into marshes, black and deep-mucked as sorcery, watching her mother come home, while she puts on her dress, and the leaves outdoors turn pale and dry. Her mother goes down into the dark of the basement to do the wash, to have a baby, to stroke the backs of silent stunned fish and become one herself—cool, so cool that she does without food, and waits, and is waiting still, until all of it blurs together, twisting into scary good smells that fill Ann's nose with damp and mold and earth.

I suppose she would tell you this was her coming of age, that autumn the beginning of a daughter's long and special rebellion against her mother, and her mother's against her. That's one sort of story.

Margaret is still ironing, but her glance says she's surprised to hear anyone admit to something *special*—between them? Her mother shakes out a shirt as she flicks Ann a look, who knows from the billowing snap that she's been found too full of bones to pick, spiny and pointed herself.

Caught at her game, telling stories, untwisting that couch's red-coiled fringe, Ann pretends her mother isn't there in her picture—the source and witness to her every word, her judge, always. The coil springs back, winds together, as if Ann had never hurt a thing, and what sort of story is that?

Cold-eyed, her mother does not smile, but in some new blur of gold, diving fleet as her mother's eye, flashing, Alex appears on the floor at Ann's side, somehow fat and diapered again, hair baby-fine. It was then Ann remembered that Alex had been a fish in her belly only a day or so ago, and that a crumb of oatmeal can tempt swimmers up out of darkness. They will show you their supple spines, their brass—they glint, breathing water alive.

THE VISITATION

Mossy McWhirter stood at the top of the stairs and peered down into the dark, weighing the odds Whizzo was down there. She didn't so much smell the damp metal and wet cement as feel it through her skin, as she eased herself down the steps. At the bottom, waiting for her eyes to readjust, she studied the cellar's corners.

The cool of the floor was creeping into her feet by the time she finally made him out. Half-hidden by cobwebs wooly with dust, he was up on the ledge near the beams—she saw him, his two yellow eyes, the hump of his outline, backlit by the single mud-spattered window.

At first she thought he was a vision—she's been troubled by these lately—thought she could see in his eye a self-possession approaching malevolence. Whizzo's meow brought the old woman to her senses. Hunting mice, she told herself. Best let him be. Yet heading back up the stairs, she couldn't help picturing again how he had looked with the window's light tippling his fur, his silhouette a halo—how the eyes had stared at her, disembodied by the dark.

Mossy, in her final days, had let go of just about everything but cats. She liked to spend mornings in tea-drinking and light housekeeping, and then read a little. And every afternoon she napped in her rocker, stroking whichever cat happened up into her lap. Now she rocked with her head tilted back, chanting, "Kits, cats, cats, kits. How many are going to St. Ives?" A child's rhythm had floated up to the rhythm of the rocker one day, unbidden, like so many other memories lately.

With eyes half-closed she followed a calico's movement as it hopped up on the back of the doilied recliner. Then she clucked at Whizzo who was sitting on an ottoman. He was looking up and seemed to be thinking about climbing the sheer curtains that hung between him and the fly bumping against the window's glass.

Sitting up straight, Mossy instructed: "Never you mind about that. Come here, my pet." She pursed her lips to make kissing noises.

Whizzo turned to look at her with golden eyes, then began to saunter toward her with an air that said he'd been planning to travel that direction anyway. From out of the kitchen came another tiger cat, and behind him a white Persian and a yellow alley cat, all curious about the lip-smacking. On the stairs coming down into the parlor, two more cat faces stared out from between banisters, while three young ones appeared at the top, rolling and biting and galloping together. Still another stretched in a patch of sun on the carpet, yawning.

There were 17 additional cats. Fourteen more of them—some days more, some days less—lived outside. Mossy regretted not being able to take in every cat that came to her door, but in spite of what the neighbors thought, she was not really crazy, and knew she could deal with only so many litter pans and hair balls. It was just that, as usual, she could deal with more than the average person.

Whizzo had been her single exception to the self-imposed indoor limit. He stood aside with an air of disinterest whenever she fought to keep the clamoring mob outside. She liked his style. It was her own.

She had to coax him in the first time, dancing a kicking fandango to keep the others out, while he took his time and strolled around the edge of the open door. Once inside, he took for granted that the best chair, the largest dish, the fondest words were for him. Whizzo—she had named him for the way he propelled himself off the porch without warning, and so quickly her eyes couldn't follow him—had one tattered ear and a half-dozen hairless crescents on his striped coat, healed-over wounds from courting days. She knew this because even now he was apt to disappear for days at a time.

Lying in bed on those nights, she sometimes heard the yowls of his mating, unearthly sounds that made the hair on her arms stand on end, but that stirred something else, too, akin to the wildness. Getting up to look out the window, she half-dreaded the source of those awful noises, and strained to see it.

"Ah, Whizzo, you're a cat's cat," she liked to say. And cats were about the only thing she admired anymore.

❧

Not so, her neighbors. The Lesters said, "Animal lover or not, there are limits." And by this they meant to cats, to old ladies, to their patience.

"Making a mess all over the neighborhood," Mr. Lester listed his grievances as he peered out the kitchen window at Mossy's side porch. "Using our garden mulch for a catbox, howling all over the neighborhood when one comes into heat."

59

"The fish smell's what gets me," said Mrs. Lester. She was referring to the fish-flavored gruel that Mossy kept bubbling on the back of her stove at all times. With so many to feed, Cat Chow was out of the question, but her pets didn't mind the homemade soup. And by now, Mossy hardly noticed the odor except when she came in from outside sometimes. "Phew!" she said then, hunching up her shoulders. In a moment, her nose was re-accustomed.

The Lesters, however, had complained to the Mayor, The Health Commissioner, Mossy's visiting nurse, and finally the district representative who had referred the case to an aide—who just that morning had sent the Lesters a letter which recommended they take it up with the Mayor or the Health Commissioner...

"He forgot the Visiting Nurses Society," Mrs. Lester said, standing up on tiptoe to read the letter over Mr. Lester's shoulder.

Mr. Lester had not got to be steward of the longshoremen local by laughing at injustice and the buck-passing of bureaucracies. Consequently he did not laugh at his wife's little joke, nor had she expected him to. "Well, I don't see what choice we have now," he said, folding the letter while he continued to stare out the window. The way he said it made Mrs. Lester think it best not to ask what exactly that might mean.

❦

When the weather warmed up, Mossy liked to take her rocker out on the side porch facing her neighbor's garden. Her mind kept casting up an odd collection of remembrances,

60

the slight ones as pungent as significant ones, so that discerning which was which seemed not to matter, was only an act in keeping with her motion: forward, backward, equidistant.

On this particular day, for no particular reason, she was remembering how her father had liked his beef cooked until it was bundles of string that grew as she chewed it. Good, he said shoveling it in.

And that made her think of the way her family said it was good how her brother died quickly, falling into the cornhusker like he did.

Now there were the old ladies at the church who came knocking for volunteers, who thought she was good because she made fourteen pumpkin pies for their silly bazaar one time, and she did it only because it had broken her Aunt Thalma's record—and good lord, what would she have done with all the pumpkins otherwise!

That last memory occurred because she was watching Mr. Lester stack runaway clubs of zucchini on his back porch. His short-hair terrier was following behind him, back and forth, sniffing at everything along the way with intense interest that never flagged, like the incessant wagging of his little tail that curled up over a back too broad for the rest of him. It was inevitable that he would be in the way at some point—Mossy had seen the whole scenario many times before—and that his yelp would frighten Lester and then embarrass him so that he whipped the dog until it cringed in apology for having gotten stepped upon.

Every time it happened, Mossy and Whizzo and a half dozen cats sat on the porch and solemnly witnessed it. But they were easily distracted by the flutter of a white cabbage butterfly or the need to straighten some wayward hair with a quick lick or a pass of the hand.

"Good Zagnut," they heard Lester praise the dog, or "Bad Zagnut," when the dog did something doggy like digging a hole. Lester couldn't just let the dog be, and Zagnut, that actor, would roll over to expose his belly, though it was certain he'd learned nothing. It was not a scene any self-respecting cat could pay attention to.

Good or bad, Mossy disliked Zagnut's undiscerning energy, the way he ran everywhere in tense lock-knee struts, wheezing with excitement, his nails tearing up the dirt. The way he always obeyed finally and came when he was called.

Still, what did it matter, all his pointless bustle, just so long as he kept to his own side of the hedge? She had more important things on her mind.

⁗

It was the next morning that Mossy discovered the first one. A white-faced gray cat lay on its side near the door when she came out for her mail, its eyes staring at an empty space on the porch. The fur near the corners of its open mouth was darkened by some fluid.

"Amelia?" said Mossy. She had named that cat for its innocent face, its pink nose. Amelia didn't stir. Only its gray, downy fur moved in the morning air, flattened and parted in places by the wind to show the immaculate skin.

At the sound of Mossy's voice, the remaining outdoor cats began collecting: some jumped down from window ledges, some appeared from underneath the porch. They climbed the front steps, or walked along the porch railing with their tails up for balance. Mossy counted them, petted those within reach, her heart pounding.

Amelia was not the first cat Mossy had lost, but she was not an old cat. And Mossy could see no mark on her body. She stooped over to touch her, and was startled at the body's cool, wooden feeling.

Standing up, she looked over at the Lester's house, not 30 feet away. The morning sun was reflected in their windows with such brilliance that she had to squint, a hand held over her eyes like a visor. No one stirred over there except for their fat, asthmatic terrier who was chained to the wrought iron railing of their landing to do his duty.

When she turned back to the shadow of the porch in Amelia's direction, her sight had trouble with the adjustment. For a moment she thought she saw a cat with overlarge ears and a circlet of gold on its head. Its eyes studied hers with an intense familiarity.

Not until the image had faded did she wonder why she felt so at ease with the creature there, never questioning its oddity, or the fact that it had wings—not until later.

She bent over too quickly, she decided, when she scooped Amelia up with her apron. And anyway, her eyes weren't so used to the sun anymore.

❧

Because she was about the business of dying, Mossy's work was remembering. Out on the porch, if she turned her head to one side, she could see her reflection in the window. It was distasteful to have to own up to the fact that frizzy white hair standing up on end, the withered face, were hers. She was eminently respectable looking; she could be anybody's great grandma, and them proud of her, too. The way the church ladies came by, expecting her to quilt and bake pies like she had always been one of them—lord!

Not that it would kill her to be circumspect for once. But then again, look at her. Good manners never saved a body from the grave. Mrs. Watt, she would say the next time the president of the Ladies Aid came by, I have been married four times and never put up with crap from anyone. Walked out when it pleased me and made my own way, and being well thought of was never something I dreamed of.

A sleek, black cat named Nefertiti stepped along the porch rail and leaped into her lap. Mossy stroked it absent-mindedly. The sky was brilliant blue. It hadn't changed a bit, Mossy thought, since the day Melvin's biplane landed in the Pritcherd's sorghum field.

"Wanna take a whirl?" he had asked her in front of everyone. Because she was pretty.

Mossy flattened back the ears of the cat, following the curve of her skull with her hand. The cat's profile reminded her of that bust of the Egyptian queen, her eyes staring and preoccupied. The Egyptians, so she had heard, once worshipped cats.

She had never been religious much, but she'd prayed that day at Pritcherd's. Because she knew why Melvin singled her out—with every kid in Twin Forks there to see him load the first mail bags and dying for what she was just offered— she felt honor bound to take the dare, and damn the scandal. Tongues could just twaddle about this the way they had over her and Leonard Murdoch, the way they did about anything she did.

She had climbed on board, feeling the canvas wobble underneath her, shaken by the palsied motor. She believed her heart might pound clear through her sternum.

"Ready?" Melvin called out to her as she slipped the goggles down over her eyes. And they started off, flattening canes under the wings, bumping up over furrows, bumping right...up...over the willows! God almighty, even now she remembered the feeling...how could this be happening?

From that moment she had wanted to fly more than she wanted to be Mrs. Leonard Murdoch or belong to the Methodist Church or keep her family's respect. So she went off with Melvin Oronsky and left Leonard flat.

Whizzo came over to sit on Mossy's feet. He looked up and studied her the way he liked to study flies in the window. Suddenly he jumped up on her lap, startling Nefertiti into flight. Purring, he bumped his head against Mossy's when she leaned down to pet him.

"Just what are you so sure of?" she asked him when he kept on staring at her unblinking eyes. "What is it you see?"

Lately she's had moments when she worried about her life. Leonard had said she was cold-hearted. Melvin accused her of using him. Well, she had taken her opportunities as they came. Was it her fault opportunities only came with men? For a while she had even been part-owner of an air circus, thanks to husband number four. And what was so bad about that?

"Red lipstick! Whiskey!" her father said the last time he saw her. And that was when her relatives were still talking to her. Only she'd outlasted them all, and maybe now they could understand what she was about, and envy her from their coffins.

"Life, Poppa!" she said to him now. "I wanted life! Don't you see how that's the thing?"

She caught a glimpse of her reflection in profile again, her one visible eye incredulous. God almighty, how could this be happening? She could ask him face to face soon enough, she could feel it.

Nefertiti was the next to turn up missing. But Mossy was not certain she was poisoned too until Orville and Eddie were both found stiff under the lilac bush. A suspicious empty tuna tin was on the ground near where they had died.

To prevent losing more, Mossy gathered in all the remaining outdoor cats—and perhaps a lucky one or two extra who happened along that day—and locked the door behind, determined to keep even Whizzo indoors until she could think of something.

Lena, the visiting nurse, thought she had gone too far. "They're getting out of hand, Mossy. A few for company, yes, I was glad to see it. But this!" She motioned toward her feet where a group sat looking up at her. Others rubbed against her stockings, curling their tails around her legs.

"I'm not one to do things halfway," answered Mossy.

"But they only make more work for you. That awful chowder you cook—"

"They like it. I'm not complaining. Suppose you stick to what you came for and take my blood pressure."

Lena pursed her lips, sighed, then opened her bag and took out the black, nylon band. "I'm only trying to help," she said, wrapping it around Mossy's arm and then squeezing the rubber bulb. "Some kids I know in the neighborhood be thrilled to help you take care of the cats."

Mossy looked at Lena who seemed about 50, her heavy arms wobbly, her bosom properly called a bosom. A regular mother hen, thought Mossy, perfect for this kind of work. Always nagging to let her install a call box for emergencies, always fussing. Lord, when she was her age, the last thing she was worried about was taking somebody else's temperature.

So then how had she wound up here? Living alone in her dumpy little house, property wrested from the last divorce years ago. No one to come calling but the Ladies Aid and the visiting nurse. Twin Forks, three states away, the Triple A Flying Circus, worlds away. Having run out of things to do and the energy with which to do them—which was how she's defined her life.

And then the first kitten turned up on her porch. What a racket! Yowling until she let it in. And somehow the word got out there in catland, and here she was on her way to St. Ives. Kits, cats, cats kits. How many die in St. Ives? Well, all of them finally, she thought with a start.

"The thing I like about cats," she said to Lena then, "is they don't need to be taken care of. That, and they have nine lives."

"Yes, that's right. That would be what you'd like about them. Maybe you think they'll lend you one of theirs. Well, one life and one cat, that's about all I can handle, thank you."

"What's it read?"

"165 over 130. Not so good, Mossy."

"I know what it means. Now watch the salt, you're going to say next, and we'd better think about a call box. All right, I've thought about it. Consider your duty done. Watch the cats on your way out."

Not long after, Mossy happened to be looking out the parlor window at Lester who was working in his cucumber patch with Zagnut at his side. Suddenly the dog froze, one foreleg in mid-air. A kitten was walking across the lawn toward them, its head bobbing above the grass as if the blades were sharp and pricking its nose, its tail straight up in back. It mewed. Mossy couldn't hear it, but she saw its mouth open, pink and spikey with little teeth.

As if cued, Zagnut sprang then, rolling over with the kitten several times before it got away in the hedge that marked the property line. Then the kitten made a second dash for the safety under Mossy's porch. The terrier, its nose to the ground, sniffed at the hedge, while Lester stood up in his garden.

Opening her door carefully, so as not to let any cats escape, Mossy came out onto her porch. She waited several minutes for the fuzzy head of the kitten to reappear, and then went down the stairs to coax it out.

"You can't go on taking in every cat in the world," Mr. Lester called out to her. "Have a little consideration for others. You've got more than your share already. It's not humane," he said.

"Don't you tell me about humane, Mr. Lester. I guess I know what you've been up to."

"Well, Mrs. McWhirter, I have tried to talk to you in the past. If you would just take some advice, give some of them cats away. There are limits to this life."

Mossy glared at him for several minutes before she

took the kitten inside and showed it to the others. There were 27 indoor cats now. Self-respecting, every one, they stared at this newest member without so much as giving away a blink about their feelings. Well, all right, she thought. It was silly. She could admit it. Sitting in her rocker, Mossy turned the kitten so she could look into its face, and then said to it: "Now what about a name for you...? Angina! Isn't that a pretty name?"

The kitten's mew pierced her heart with its thin, tiny assertion.

That night, in the floating moments just before sleep, the cat she had seen on the porch, the one with the circlet of gold on its head, reappeared to her. It was close enough to her face to be sitting on her chest, but it seemed to be suspended above her somehow. It was large and its fur was thick as mink. It seemed sprinkled with silvery talc or powdered diamonds, or else it had some wonderful infestation of phosphorescent fleas.

But then again, she thought, perhaps it was just her eyes seeing spots from having just turned out the table lamp next to her bed. As if in answer to this doubt, the cat blinked its eyes slowly, and Mossy felt the sweep of its eyelids in her soul.

She supposed it was her soul.

Mossy couldn't find Whizzo the next morning. She searched everywhere—not for the first time, he was like that.

But this time, something told her, something told her....

As a last resort she descended the poorly lit stairs down into the cellar. She felt a draft on her legs and noticed the light seemed especially bright pouring in through the window—had someone washed it? No. Broken out a pane!

Mossy put one hand over her mouth. Two lumps of fur lay on the ledge near the window, looking like small, discarded coats. She pulled a stepstool over to the window and climbed it, shaking a little. It was Iris and Piper Cub—

Oh, Cubby," she said to the young short hair, remembering she last saw him trailing after Whizzo, trying o bite his tail.

The following week, almost as an aside, Mossy gave the new kitten, Angina, to Lena the visiting nurse, and asked her to tell the children that she wanted homes for the others. It was not that she no longer loved the cats. Quite the contrary, she told herself.

Lena interpreted all this to mean that Mossy had resigned herself to the inevitable. She believed that people had a sense about when their time had come, and without asking, brought in an emergency call box for the table next to Mossy's rocker.

But in fact, Mossy had remembered that down on the ledge of her Michigan basement, where she kept things she knew she would never use again, she still had an old bag of herbicide. Left over from the days when the Triple A was on its last leg, doing odd jobs like spraying for the utility lines, she judged it was still strong enough to wither Lester's zucchini and flatten his tomato plants. She relished the thought of seeing them yellowed with their leaves curling, dropping fruit that was still green and knurled.

On a night when dark skies were promised, and after she had fed her few remaining cats, Mossy mixed the Seismal with water in a ratio dozens of times stronger than the label recommended. By the time she let herself out into the night air, there was lightning deep in the clouds, and a rumble of faraway thunder.

She was dressed in a navy crepe dress that made her seem part of the shadows, and dark chenille slippers muffled her footsteps. To disguise her white hair, she had on her old leather flying helmet, still supple enough to hug her skull.

She stood watching the back of the Lesters' house, saw a single light in the bathroom go on, then off. The house was dark. She squeezed through the hedge and into the garden, the crickets singing in see-sawing rhythms the whole while, oblivious to what she carried.

When she was nearly in line with her own porch door, she began to adjust the top of her plastic bottle. It would only spray when the nozzle setting was just right, and it had never worked very well. She fingered it, watching the Lesters' house.

A light came on, a moment passed, and then the back door opened. Mossy's heart lurched at the thought of being discovered. But no, she soon heard the door close again. She saw a shadowy figure on the landing. Zagnut! His body dropped to the ground. Almost immediately he began to bark.

Now her heart was pounding—lord! She would drop over dead before she could finish the job. She stooped over, but Zagnut wasn't barking at her, there was something else.

Mr. Lester stuck his head out, shouted at Zagnut to shut up, and closed the door again, without detecting her. At the sound of the door slamming, a cat—by god, it's Whizzo!—

shot out from under a bush to bound up the trunk of a crab apple tree near the garden.

He's been off courting in the next county, Mossy said to herself, smiling their shared secret, watching while he settled in a lower branch just out of reach, to taunt the little dog.

Zagnut gave several sharp barks that made him hop backwards a little each time. He put his nose to the ground next, and began sniffing in Mossy's direction. Tense, Mossy dropped the bottle. Zagnut looked up, his ears pointed toward her.

"Zaggy. Come here, little Zaggy," Mossy whispered, hating the sweet tone she was using. The dog wagged his tail. He wouldn't give her away after all. He liked it when she was in the garden. Mossy could see that Whizzo was watching the two of them with that steady, golden stare.

She reached down for the bottle to find that the top had come loose and a puddle had formed on the ground near the nozzle. She began screwing the nozzle back on, and then tried squeezing the trigger, but nothing came out.

Damn thing. Get out of here, dog, sniffing around here, get away. There, finally. She pumped and pumped, and finally the mist came shooshing out, over the bushy zucchini, the tall, stake-tied tomatoes. She pumped until the white rags that tied the vines were soaked and hanging limp, dripping their surfeit into tiny puddles on the ground.

But no, wait—that slurping noise. Mossy turned to see Zagnut was lapping up the puddle of Seismal that had spilled when she dropped the bottle. She slapped at his broad back, felt sickened at the warmth of his slick fur. This wasn't supposed to happen, get out of here, stupid dog—

"Zagnut!" called Mrs. Lester from the porch. "Come here, Zaggy."

The dog straightened up at his mistress's call, and ran for the back door. Mossy watched him, waiting for his legs to snarl up or start dragging, for him to keel over just before he reached her. But instead he hopped onto the landing and looked up at Mrs. Lester as she held the door open for him.

"Come in, sweetheart," she chirruped. The door closed, the light went off again.

Mossy would have to imagine what happened next, and that tamped it down deeper in her: the rattling cough, the stiffening limbs, the Lesters' panic at being unable to explain his death—Good Zagnut, Bad Zagnut, it didn't seem to matter.

She was waiting to hear some wail of grief for that miserable, cringing dog. Lord! She was more than waiting, she was longing for it, she wanted to throw back her head and join the howl. Not just for him—for herself, for this leveling.

There was a numbness in her hand. Her eyes were blurring a little. And perhaps because of that she thought she could see Whizzo beginning to levitate—right off the apple branch as she watched.

Or maybe he was just growing larger. There seemed to be flashes of light inside his fur, like the heat lightning in the clouds overhead. And something in his eyes was seeking her out, and connected finally, inviting her to shake hands with herself and begin a long, long acquaintance.

74

WHAT HAPPENED AT WANDA'S PLACE

The stretch of highway just past the farm and on the way into Nortonville, the nearest town, went straight through some of the flattest, poorest land in the state, all planted to orchards. Apples and peaches, row after row, that's all you could see for a good ten miles until you came to Wanda's Place on the north side of M-160. It was well before the John Deere Tractor place, there were more orchards to drive through before you finally got to Nortonville, but Wanda's Place was the first sign that said you might actually get somewhere if you kept on driving.

It was nothing much, that's the god's truth. Four years before, the Pulaskys had settled in and tried to make the place go. Wanda and her husband Bill had painted the cinder blocks gray and then because the building was completely square and plain and begged for something fancy, they had stenciled orange stars near the door and next to the glass brick windows. Last winter, Russell had helped them add on a kind of entryway made of ribbed fiberglass panels an aquamarine color. He'd been happy to do it. The place was more like a friend's house than a bar, or like a private club, with just a few even knowing about Wanda's—on a good Saturday night, maybe a dozen, and always the same crowd. It was why Russell liked Wanda's Place and hung out there when he could. It was comfortable.

But no way to run a business, he guessed, and he

couldn't say he blamed Bill and Wanda for trying something new to grab up customers. Talk about your free publicity, the whole town was in an uproar, letters to the editor, and photos of Wanda and Bill saying they had to make a living somehow, didn't they? And ministers threatening to close down the place, and even the kids talking about it at school, he guessed, judging from the giggling his nephew and his friends were doing—and why not? The little guy was old enough to read the papers, wasn't he?

It wasn't as if this was typical for Russell. It was Dwayne who had to go and be so goddamn hot to trot. The two of them had been sitting there alone in the bar with Wanda, and she let on she had some big secret to tell, and finally she let on about Bill hiring two girls out of Grand Rapids to come and dance topless on weekends and maybe draw up the crowd from South Bend, Indiana, where they had them topless places everywhere. It wasn't anything anymore. Why they even had a bottomless place in South Bend, and X-rated movie houses close to Buchanan and North Haven. You could see such stuff just about anywhere but Nortonville.

Old Dwayne had been beside himself. "Oh Jesus," he said. "Did I ever tell you about the time I saw this show in Chicago once? Damnedest thing I ever saw. Damned if she didn't get those things to swing around in circles, first one way you know, and then the other? And then, I swear to god, like this!" he said and twirled his fingers in opposite directions in front of his chest to show how awe-inspiring it had been.

And then first thing Russell knew, Dwayne had volunteered them both for the welcome wagon. You know these farmers don't know how to act, he said to Wanda. The poor girls would need some protection, wouldn't they? Oh yeah, Wanda answered, but just who is it that's gonna protect them from you two? And it was her saying that, clinched it for him. The way she included him in the same class as Dwayne: the way she said, who was going to protect those girls from you and that one, and she gestured toward Russell who was caught up short in a swig, and stopped in mid-gulp with foam on his lip.

"Look, you don't have to worry," Dwayne had told Russ more than once. "Now take me for instance. I'm short, got a big nose. Big nose. Course I got all my hair and lots of people say I got what women call bedroom eyes, no shit, but still, I'm telling you, there is no reason why girls should go for me and not for you. I mean, the word is confidence. I go in and I look at a girl, and I think a her like a ripe peach you just have to tap, like so, and it falls right into your hand, just fills out your hand with that ripe little round ass. Man it's confidence, that's all."

✑

Russell was so busy thinking, it seemed like no time before he was pulling into the back of Wanda's Place, bouncing through the ruts in the gravel to park where he always did, near the backdoor where the beer racks were stacked. And Jesus, there it was. The van, just like Dwayne had promised. Candy-apple red, flashing glitter like a race-car, a bulged out porthole on the side. Even the picture of a water-skier splashing along on silver enamel, his pelvis thrust out going full throttle, straight for it.

Russ pulled in next to it, turned the key in the ignition, stared ahead for a moment with both hands on the wheel, and then turned to look down into the van's cockpit. That's what it was alright, a roaring cockpit: turbo-tilt seats, all in plush, a wrap-around console and dials that wouldn't quit and just like he'd pictured it: red shag on the floor and clear up the walls, and further back, a table, two long couches—

Jesus H. Christ—the thought raced through his mind— he was really gonna have to go through with it. And suddenly he could see himself, lounging on red shag, a gorgeous blond next to him. He was staring into her eyes while he poured her drink so the wine came just to the brim of a long-stemmed glass and shimmied there. You are such a beautiful woman, he would say, and watch her red lips part, see the tip of her wet little tongue.

Oh shit. He could never say all that straight, not without mumbling or spilling something. But dammit all, he could sure as hell try, couldn't he?

He got out of the truck, slammed the door, and headed right for the back door of Wanda's without so much as a sideways glance, grabbing on to the screen door handle like it was a life-ring. The vent fan overhead was whirring so loud he couldn't hear himself think, and when he opened the door, it sent a rush of air like warm, stale beer into his face. A soon as his eyes adjusted to the dimness, he headed for the bar. The only light in the place was shining down on tiers of whiskey bottles that always reminded him of a church's pipe organ made of glass there behind the bar.

Dwayne was seated on a barstool at the counter and called out to him as he crossed the dance floor. "Hey, Russell! Say now, get a look at you!"

He reached up without thinking and smoothed down his still-damp bangs.

Dwayne had pulled out a barstool for him and was lighting up a cigarette. "You look a little nervous," he said, and inhaled deeply so that the cigarette gleamed in the half-light. Then he blew streams of smoke out his nose.

"Lemme have one of those," said Russell, and tapped the end of it on the bar before he put it into his mouth.

"I thought you quit," Dwayne said.

"Yeah," he answered. "You just look so bad-ass though."

He took a drag and then he laughed a little to show he was cool, silent and hunched over, like he was enjoying the biggest, bitterest joke in the world. He ordered a draft, and sat silent then, sipping his beer, while he looked around the place. Bill and Wanda had fixed it up some. They'd moved the dozen small tables over to one end to make more room for the dancers, and put little candles in red glasses on each of the tables.

Bill and Wanda had also slid the two pin-ball machines together close in one corner, and nearby, had built a plywood platform to make do as a stage. The smell of new lumber wafted in and out with the stale beer smell, the cigarettes.

After a moment, Russell noticed an added touch: they had put a revolving colored light, one left over from the days when aluminum Christmas trees were the thing, on the floor next to the stage. He motioned toward it, saying lamely, "Place looks real nice."

Bill, standing behind the bar, answered with a grunt and a nod, while he peered into a glass, wiping it out. Wanda just kept on sponging the perfectly clean bar. They were all feeling it, Dwayne was too, never mind that smirky smile of his. Every once in a while, one of them would try saying something nice or something meant to be funny and the words would just hit the floor with a thud, and finally they all just shut up.

⚬⚬⚬

Russell was just about to order another beer when the front door swung open and a little guy appeared in the crack of light. He squinted into the dark, but even with his face screwed up, Russell could see he was a stranger. He had long stringy hair and a beard, so he sure as hell wasn't from anywhere around Nortonville. He seemed to be checking them all out, and then he opened the door wider and called out, "Okay, this must be it."

Two women in full-length coats, carrying train cases, came in through the door he held open for them. Russell felt his heart leap a little when he caught sight of the first one's face: she was pretty. No knockout, maybe, what you call a dish-water blonde. But except for her posture, which was round-shouldered, and the way her arms hung limp at their sides, Russell approved. She had freckles. This made him feel better somehow.

As soon as she set her train-case down, she crossed her arms over her stomach, and stood slumped over, watching them all from under the cover of her bangs. Russell began to feel nervous watching her eyes. Her glance darted around the room, stopping briefly at faces, but only for a fraction of a second before they came back to the face of the bearded man.

Behind her a stocky girl had come in. Unlike the first woman, she moved with confidence, exuberant as a fat kid at a barbeque. Russell sensed right away that something about her was out of kilter. Her mouth was too big, it gaped open in a grin that looked as if it had forgotten what was funny. Her eyes were vague and unfocused.

"You Bill?" the man with the beard said and he came forward extending a hand. "Wanda? Glad to meetcha. I'm Skip Blatchford. This here's Tina," he said, motioning to the slump-shouldered girl, "and this gal here is Marcia Lorraine."

The fat girl came forward and giggled, a little too loudly.

"I'm Marcia Lorraine," she repeated in the voice of a nine-year-old. Russell looked over at Dwayne. He was slowly lowering his cigarette to an ashtray. He was turning gray.

Marcia came closer to Russell. "Hi," she said and giggled again. "You're cute." Her mouth gaped open and her tongue, too large and swollen, spilled over her teeth and protruded slightly. "Whatcha drinking? Can I have some?" She didn't wait for an answer but grabbed the mug roughly and slurped down the last of Russell's beer, leering at him until he thought his blood would run cold. She wiped the foam from her bottom lip finally and giggled again.

"You the two Bill told me about? Gonna help keep things in line?" Skip was talking to Dwayne and Russell now.

"Uh, yeah. That's right," Dwayne managed to say, still staring at Marcia Lorraine.

"That's good," Skip said. "We might need you before the night's over. Things are liable to get lively."

Marcia Lorraine kept on looking at Russell with bold, glassy eyes. Like some pervert baby, he thought with a start. He looked down at his mug, tapped his finger against it. In a moment he felt her hand on his shoulder, heavy, insistent. She bent over to peer into his face, coming closer than was decent, coming close enough he could smell the tang of her sweat, the heat of her breath. "Hey," she said. "Hey. You wanna see me do my dance?"

The way she said that, it was like his nephew little Walt asking, did he want to see him ride his bike with no hands, did he want to see a backwards somersault?

"That's not a bad idea," Skip said. "I like to have them rehearse a little, you know—get the hang of the place. You mind?" He didn't wait for Bill or Wanda to answer. Russell could see they were both in a state of shock too, hadn't realized what they bargained for in Marcia Lorraine. Skip herded the two women back toward the rest room and as soon as they were out of sight, Dwayne practically vaulted himself into the stool beside Russell.

"I'll be goddamned," he said in a hoarse whisper. "The one's a retard. A mental case. If my dog had a face like that, I'd make it walk backwards!"

"You change in there now," Skip called out in the hallway, and then sauntered back toward the bar. Now that he knew who they were, he was feeling friendly, confiding in them like they were old friends from way back. "They're sisters," he said, nodding toward the restroom. "They don't look or act nothing alike, but they're sisters. Tina's my old lady and she had this soft spot for the kid, you know—I didn't want her, but turns out it's that Marcia Lorraine really packs 'em in. Dumb as a carp, she is, but you watch."

On cue, as if she'd been introduced, the bathroom door burst open and whacked against the wall with a bang. Marcia Lorraine came out, her thighs rubbing together as she walked, her knees and calves looking too small to hold up her weight. She had nothing on but a blue satin bikini bottom. Its elastic cut into soft flesh that was white and dimpled with fat; her breasts were enormous.

"You watch me," she called out to Russell, mortifying him with her favor, and then she walked over to the new wood platform. Russell felt the awful-est confusion, watching her great, hulking movement. He had a tingly sensation all over and he couldn't stand it. He couldn't stand looking at her and hearing her little girl's voice, "Watch me now."

By this time, Tina had come out of the bathroom too and was following Marcia to the stage in front of them. She was unhealthy skinny, Russell thought. If she'd been one of his livestock he'd have fed her supplements, wormed her, maybe shot her if she didn't get better, though it would have broke his heart. She walked with her shoulders curved in, close as she could come to modesty, her tits flattened cones.

She glanced several times at Skip, who urged her forward with a nod of his head, and then once on stage, she assumed a distant stare that went right out over the men's heads, focused where the walls met the ceiling. She kept it there while Skip put on a record. Russell recognized it was something from Saturday Night Fever.

Their two bodies and the way they moved were so different that part of Russell wanted to laugh; but on the other hand, if they weren't gorgeous, they were naked, and the part of him in his pants said to shut up and get serious. The women began shuffling in time to the music, warming up. And then Skip noticed the Christmas tree light on the floor and plugged it in. It swept over them in triangles of color—red, blue and green—rippling with a movement that accented theirs, making them seem more like a dream than real people.

"Good idea," Skip commented as he sat down next to him. "Hey, come on," he yelled in their direction then. "Let's see some action, let's see some smiles."

Russell felt sick at the way Tina looked at him with that quick glance, and then smiled, just a little, while she turned her gaze back to that spot above their heads. She was managing not to move much.

But that Marcia Lorraine! She was beaming before Skip said anything and there was nothing faked about it; she was flinging her arms around, kicking her legs up, paying no attention to the music at all, but moving to some odd, inward beat. And every time she turned around, her flesh wiggled and jiggled with a life of its own, doing triple time, going around and around. If he'd seen that fat behind on some old lady in downtown North Haven, he'd have laughed, jammed an elbow in Dwayne's side and entertained him with a moo. But this girl had him breathing quick, and the colors kept on going around, and the music kept on beating. Marcia Lorraine bent her knees and started dipping and swaying, so her breasts swung alarmingly from side to side, still faster and faster, until Dwayne was up on his feet. "Chicago," he yelled. "It's just like Chicago."

And the colors whirled round and around, red, blue, green, keeping time with the music, keeping time with the pulsing in Russell's head. Only Russell couldn't stand it, couldn't stand hearing Dwayne chant "Go baby, go baby, go," because Russell was starting to shout too, he shouted, "Just like Chicago! Oh Jesus! Look at her go!"

And then it was over. A scratching noise came over the speaker and that was the end.

Russell had been so hypnotized by Marcia Lorraine's

performance he was almost surprised to see Tina getting down off the platform. She took one of the kimonos that Skip was offering to them. He bent over, pulled the plug on the Christmas tree light. "Hey, look, honey," Russell heard him say to her. "You gotta get into this more."

She nodded, folding her arms across the front of the kimono. She glanced at him, fluttering her eyelids, nervous, and then glanced away.

Marcia was waddling over to see Russell, tying the belt of her robe. "Did you like it??" she asked, coming too close to him all at once again. "I do it pretty good, don't I?" she said. "Skip, he taught me how to do a lot of that stuff. I had a man give me a necklace once after he saw me dance, he liked me so much. I lost it now, I can't show you, but it was so pretty. I cried and cried when I lost it..."

He watched her, amazed; she was a child again.

"I liked your dance a lot, Marcia Lorraine," Dwayne said over Russell's shoulder. "I never saw a girl dance like you before."

"Honest?" she said, and she giggled, her queer gash of a smile growing wider.

"Oh yeah, baby. You do things to me."

He came around Russell's barstool and stood close to her, so that Russell could have heard if he'd cared to listen. But he didn't have to hear to understand—it was Dwayne Burford, great American lover at work, and that horny baby-girl, whispering and giggling about the van out back. Maybe she wouldn't be so ready to cozy up to him, if Russell told her what Dwayne had said about her. But he didn't want to hurt her feeling, and anyway, what he'd said was—

Russell looked up from his third beer to see that Tina

was staring at him. Her eyes were hazel, he noticed, now that she held them in a steady gaze. But as soon as she realized he was looking back, she fluttered her lashes and looked at something else, the way she had with Skip when he'd bawled her out.

∽

Soon after that, Tiny Higgins and the guys from the paper mill, and Phil Wooley and Stuart Rheims and a whole bunch of others Russell didn't even recognize, began pouring in, getting ready for the big event at Wanda's Place. Skip and Dwayne rushed the girls back to the bathroom until it was time. It was a sure thing the crowd was going to be rowdy. They were already buzzing like yellow jackets swarming a new hive, laughing, yelling every so often, hey, over here! You sonofabitch, how you been?

By the time Russell was on his fifth beer, the place was packed. Some big guy had draped one arm over his shoulder, was hollering over the din into his ear so that everyone around them could hear: "I hear you got the inside track, you know these girls..." And Russell was cool, nodded yes, it was so—thought, at last, he was in the same class as Dwayne. He was hot shit, he was, only all of it was chicken shit.

And then Skip went over and plugged in the colored lights and it was dark and the shouts got louder and the crowd began clapping and whistling for the girls to come out. The big man headed for a better seat and Dwayne slipped in beside Russell, leaned over and whispered in his ear, "Our ole buddy Skip says that maybe something can be arranged with little Tina and you, what do you say? Tina and you, and me and Marcia Lorraine? Hey, don't worry, he says they do it all the time. Didn't I tell you? There ain't nothing you can't do if you got you a van!"

He laughed and Russell watched the lights play on his face, watched that smart-ass smile of his and thought how he'd love to push his teeth down his throat—red, blue, green—

"Hey Russell, where you going?" Dwayne called after him. "Hey you can have Marcia Lorraine if that's what you want!"

The back door slammed behind him and he was standing outside, the cool night air rising up in his face in damp waves. He could hear the clapping now by the thump of boots on the floor, mugs on the tables. The van was close by; its red looked purplish in the dark.

What in hell was wrong with him? Dwayne and those others'd never let him live it down, lettin' his feelings get in the way at a time like this. Christ, Dwayne'd just take the both of them poor defenseless girls on, and then have twice the story to tell. Didn't matter to him.

It galled Russell, how hollow and lonely and full of envy he felt. It was not the sort of reward he would have imagined for being a better man than Dwayne. He reached for the handle on his truck, thinking, no doubt he'd kick himself in the morning. And at that, Russell had to laugh a little to himself, silent and hunched over, he had to laugh at the biggest, bitterest joke in the world.

WALLS

That hum, hear it?

I sit forward on the edge of the couch, spine stiffened, and turn my head slowly to peer into all the corners of the room, filled with shadows in this half-light. The kitchen opens into a galley off the front room, and I can see something looming there.

It's my new frost free refrigerator: antique almond with pebbled surface to camouflage fingerprints and mayonnaise smears and other signs of life. The Freon gurgles and I listen for a while, then clear my throat to make sure it is really the refrigerator making that sound and not me, strangling.

Then my couch intrudes into the silence, so heavy, so real, that it frightens me and my heart speeds up. I feel it pound against my chest. But it's a couch, not a hulking body, crouched, waiting.

Lake Michigan out my window, an extra $35 a month it costs me for the view. Between my window and the setting sun there is only a pole with an electric conduit, hanging there like a python silhouetted against the coral-colored watersky. One pool of glowing color at this time of evening in the summer, no line to mark the horizon.

It's what I stared at like my life depended on it, colors fading very quickly as the sun submerged, and I remember I watched the light disappear and me with it.

Over there. The phone? I've left it off the hook. I do every night now. The receiver hangs from a length of cord suspended just above my no-wax floor. It hangs without motion, but in my mind I see it bounce, hear it crash against the cabinets as it plummets to the floor, and me going with it, falling into a time warp, falling, falling—

No, god, no—

Other times it used to shriek in the clear black night, calling me back from hills of iridescent flowers and molten mountains and kisses from an earth-warm mouth opened against mine—Awakened, I would shrug into a robe, shaking the images from me, and stumble across cold floors to where real nightmares waited.

"Hello? Hello?"

Silence.

"Hello? Who is this?"

Silence.

I would feel a cool breath of sweat along my lower back. "If you don't answer me, I'm going to hang up."

And silence.

Every time it was the same. I would bang the receiver down—Creep! What do they get out of that! And then stand in the dark, watching for the smallest movement, or some sound to give shape to the terror.

And then finally I would grope my way back to my bed in the dark, because if I turned on the lights, he'd be able to see me, wouldn't he? Know that he'd frightened me? How do I know where he called from? Who was he? He could be anywhere, anyone.

So leave the lights off. Go back under the sheets to dream again, only now with something in pursuit, something with claws and brassy scales and a snout with a flicking tongue. I run in slow motion, gravity snaring my feet, awaken when the thing touches me.

Even at that, I used to count myself lucky because silence was the worst for me. There was Amy with her auburn hair and pale lashes and those eyes that looked watery even when she wasn't scared and ashamed. She got calls sometimes too. Which of us hadn't?

"—and then he said some things."

"What, Amy? What did he say?"

"Oh, things—things about my—he said, 'pretty pussy, pretty red pussy.' That's what scares me, you know? Like he knows I'm a redhead, I'm not just some number out of the book."

"Oh, coincidence, that's all. Don't worry," I said, not telling her how scared it made me to watch her eyes widen.

"How could he know?"

"He's guessing. He's seen you in the halls, at work or something..."

"I'm careful to draw the shades, how could he get that idea about me—?"

"It's not your fault!"

"—I never even look at men in my building."

"That's the trouble, you look too scared, and they spot you for a mark. They don't pick on women who aren't afraid of them."

"But I am afraid," she said to me.

∞

She was right, believing it wouldn't make any difference. I should have paid more attention to the way their eyes feel so heavy, pulling your vision down to your feet. They stare when you walk by, you catch them looking at you over the top of a menu, or watching you get out of your car before you've had the chance to pull your skirt down. You're supposed to feel complimented, and I guess that's the part that weighs heaviest. That sometimes I was complimented. And full of questions, wondering, what is it they see? What is this thing that makes me female and in power and powerless?

Kathy always dressed like an executive and had all the answers, making a fist in the safety of the cafeteria at break time. "We've got to stand up for ourselves. Women. Together. Forget those bastards."

But we'd all seen her at parties when she had a few drinks under her belt. She wanted them to love her. She knew what it took.

And there was Marilyn, the prettiest one in our group. Conceited about it, but charming just the same because she pretended it didn't please her.

"You see? He's doing it again."

"What?"

"He's sitting over there where I have to look at him and he's staring at me—no, don't turn around, he'll know that I told you to look."

"So what," said Kathy. "You half sound like you're flattered. Let's all stare back at him. There's four of us and one of him. We've gotta fight back instead of putting up with that kind of crap."

"Kathy, come on."

"No, no—don't," Marilyn said. "I can't. Just ignore him. Maybe he'll stop. I could just sit with my back to him so I can't see him staring."

"That's nuts. Why should you rearrange your life? He's the creep. Walk up to him and ask him what his problem is—ask him if he wants to fuck you or something?"

"Kathy! She can't do that!"

"Why not?" Kathy said, narrowing her eyes at the man.

None of us explained it. We all knew the answer already. No matter where we'd been brought up, we'd all been girls together. We knew what to do and what not to do.

Don't you use the f-word, like that.

Cover your knees, dear, don't sit like a boy—

Darling, she's much too old for you to wrestle with! You might hurt her female parts—be careful—

Girls are more delicate, that's why you can't just—

And now girls will be excused for a special movie—a Kotex movie, someone sniggers—

And remember the summer matinee? Always a group of farm workers on the street with their greasy hair and bold eyes, muttering delicious dirty words at us as we passed by? Even then we knew enough to walk home six blocks out of the way. Otherwise you'd be asking for it. You didn't want to act like you were asking for it, or they would give it to you and feel entitled. There were rules, unspoken but they were there. And there were others—

Never speak to strangers—

Cross your legs carefully—

Stare ahead with your eyes fixed—

And for heaven's sake, don't lift your arms to straighten your hair, exposing the soft white underarms— and shave it, keep it baby soft.

And don't lead them on. Remember? Your momma told you—they can't help what they feel for us. Mostly they're harmless. They beg for our mercy. They pay us homage. Nevermind we never asked for it. And bowing low before us, gentlemen, they rise to catch their noses on our skirts, and send us messages with their eyes that say, I want you for my queen, you slut.

A young girl is standing in line in front of me, waiting to get on the roller coaster like the rest of us. She has clean long hair and freckles, little breasts just beginning to pout. Her tee-shirt is pink, its scooped neck trimmed with ribbon. She is careful to keep her eyes cast down as she shifts her weight from one foot to the other. Occasionally she looks up at the white trellis of the ride.

A group of boys is ahead of us and they keep glancing back at her, exchanging looks between them. Then they duck their heads together, laughing, and look back over their shoulders at her while she pretends to ignore them. I watch her face redden, and imagine a group of girls her age singling out a young boy, making his face sting just because that's just the way it is.

But that's not the way it is. Not everywhere. Not all the time.

"Hey, getta load that ass... them jugs... naw, that

don't count. Bumpin' her tits in a crowd ain't first base, don't gimme that…"

We couldn't hear them. But we heard them. We heard them all the time. And she and I did the only thing we could. We kept our faces proud and turned away, imagined ivy growing up the trellis, its white as pretty as a picket fence around our gingham houses. We pretended we didn't know they were talking about us, not us—

"No, please, god no," I said. "Why do you have to do this? I don't understand. Look at you, you don't have to have it this way, you could have girls—

cunts
sluts
bitches
whores
quims
"Please. Please."

❧

So every night I sit here trying to figure it out. You live in a nice apartment with a chain latch on the door and a garbage disposal in the sink. And you think you know all the rules and you think you know a nice face when you see one. And when he says, "Could I help you with the groceries?" you say, "Thank you."

I said, "Thank you."

I sit here with the light out, watching shadows fill the corners of the room, glad for darkness. I wish I could be a piece of furniture like my rocker. Stock still while the dark erases it. Not to think anymore, not to have to think about

it or try to make sense out of it, not to be human flesh and
blood—

Crusted in the corner of my mouth. Blood. Proof of my
battle—

"—You gotta put up a fight—"

I did, Kathy, I did. I think I did, please believe me.

"—Bust his balls," she'd said.

But I did, I tried, "—oh no, don't do that, I'll scream, I'll
scream, oh please—"

"—I'd kick his tool to the moon, turn him into an opera
star before I'd ever let him—"

"Okay, okay, I'll do what you say, just don't use that on
me, okay. Just put that away. See, I'm being nice,"—oh god,
oh god, don't think about that, think about something else,
think about work tomorrow, think about lunch, what'll you
have for lunch, look at the refrigerator, glowing in the dark
like some big ghost, think about anything but—

the way his zipper sounds,

like a long rip—

while he watches you, that young man with the
clean hair, the nice teeth—"That looks heavy. Can I help
you with it?"

"Thank you," I said. Oh, come on, baby, you knew
better than that, letting some stranger in the door?—But no,
I thought I knew him. Didn't I know him? Didn't I see him
around the building? I thought he lived here in the complex,
he looked nice—

"Take it off," he said, and you let your bra flutter down
like angel wings and covered your eyes so you wouldn't have to
see what you heard: the clank of a belt buckle hitting the floor,
the flop of clothes that sounded like wounded birds landing.

You felt a jab of his hand and you looked up to see him naked from the waist down, and he is standing with a knife in one hand, down next to his other weapon—

"G'down," he says, and shoves you with his hand again—he is rough—and you look behind you to see where you can sit most gracefully, but there is no chair close by.

"I said get down," and he shoves you so hard that you land on the floor, flat on your backside, your legs splayed open so that you gather them quickly and fold them at the knees to cover yourself.

"Not like that," he says, pushing your shoulder, and it becomes very clear now what he means—come on, baby, you knew all along what he was after, you were asking for—but now you know, you know there is no escape and you turn your face toward the window and you cry and you whimper and you—

"Stop it!" he says.

and you can't and you can't

and you can't—breathe! My god—he's pushing something into your face. Your coat. He's going to smother you, he will kill you now, you should have fought him—

"Bust his balls, you gotta kick that bastard—"

What is he doing? Crushing me, crushing me, jamming his hand up between my legs, clawing up into me, oh god, let it be over please let it be—

∽

I sit in the dark with my heart pounding, staring at the wall across from me. Or staring at the place where a wall used to be. It's so dark now I can't see anything but the tiny flashes of color in my own eyeball.

My foot brushes against something under the couch and I jump a little, startled, until I remember what it is: the coat he put over my face. I left it rumpled on the floor where I flung it the moment I heard the door close behind him with a soft click. I remember drinking in the air, feeling giddy to be alive until I remembered what life had just given me. I couldn't bear to pick up the coat. I kicked it under the couch and left it there.

But really, it's what I think about sitting here in the dark at night. The coat part. I can't figure it out. None of it really, but the coat part especially. That he couldn't stand to watch my face, it means something.

"—please, don't do this, you look like a nice person, not the sort who would do this. Look at me, I'm begging you—"

That's when he covered my face. Maybe I looked too real. And he had to take that away from me first, before he could take the rest away with his prick. And somehow that makes him more human. And less human. Because, god help him, he did it anyway.

In my mind he does it over and over. And even in my memory, from back before I ever laid eyes on him—He's been doing it—

THE PASSING OF MCCLUSKY

Ever since he first heard McClusky had passed away, Doc Garren must have replayed that scene in his head a hundred times: McClusky's beefy hand, with its fringe of reddish hair on each finger, reaching up and handing him the prescription bottle still warm from his touch. And McClusky's face—Doc could see it plain as if he were still alive. Cheeks packed plump under fine-pored skin, teeth white and even, smiling up at him—who could say it wasn't a shame the man had to die that way? Doc Garren'd be the first to say so.

"The usual, Doc," McClusky said, and the old man— not really a doctor, but a pharmacist in a starch-stiffened smock replaying this memory in his head now, over and over again—took the amber vial from McClusky's hand, saying "Good game you bowled the other night."

And every time he remembered the last he'd seen of McClusky alive, Doc seemed to recall how the light had shone in through the drugstore window behind him, igniting colors in apothecary jars. It grew brighter every time he imagined it, the light's rays longer, reaching farther and farther back until finally he saw it hit the mirror in back of the soda fountain, watched it bounce colors off the beveled glass edges as brilliant as the red and blue dyed water in the jars.

All this was part of his memory of that scene. Though

he told himself he couldn't really have seen all that—not at the moment—with his head bowed down to watch his hands fill the amber tube with little white pills. He couldn't have seen the light and the colors and the mahogany-pillared mirror, as much as he loved them, if he'd been doing what he should have: checking and rechecking both the dosage and the name—10 milligrams Turgidaphene—watch the spelling, not Turphedizine—10 milligrams taken daily, just like always. McClusky, too heavy for his own good, too robust in his living, had a heart condition even at his age. Sad thing.

Doc Garren counted the pills onto a square of paper— an old-time method—that formed a chute down into the vial when he held it up to send the pills tumbling in like a truck loading a coal bin. Then he closed the top with the latest child-proof cap—one of his few concessions to new products being touted in Today's Pharmacy Marketing Magazine, dropped off by the wholesaler. Doc hated the magazine. The cap was required by law.

Not that anyone could accuse Doc of not being concerned with safety. He would dare anyone to say that to his face. For 43 years he had cranked the awning of Garren's Drugstore down each morning, up each evening—loving the chore, loving the chance to go out on the sidewalk in his white smock and feel the air on his bare arms while he turned the handle of the awning, looking to his left, to his right.

This was his town, he thought, taking the storefronts in with one quick look that would notice anything out of the ordinary. These were his people: Mrs. Lindell with arthritis and a cane... Jack Bundy with high blood pressure... Titus Whitmore with the gout. Even Becky Prentice who got the pill (and her mother didn't know—it'd kill her if she did)—even Becky came to Garren's 'cause she knew she could trust old Doc. They all trusted Doc. They all loved Garren's Drugstore.

True, business had dropped off some since the new Walgreen's moved in down the other end of town. Blakely was all of four blocks long, hardly big enough for two drugstores. Still those who'd been doing business with Doc were faithful to keep coming back. Just like he was faithful to them. Just like he tried to make them feel good every time they came through that door.

The bell overhead would ring. The customer—this one's Lindy Miller, tendency toward kidney-stones—stands for a moment in the rectangle of light pouring in through the window onto the floor, stands there waiting for Doc to call out, "Miss Miller! What can I do for you?"

No, those who really cared about where they went and how they conducted their business, they kept coming back to Garren's. Lord knows he didn't have one-cent sales, or mail out flyers addressed to Occupant. He sold Hallmark cards, but damned if he was going to sell Hallmark jewelry and Hallmark Christmas ornaments and Hallmark toilet-seat covers, for pete's sake.

He sold bandages, heating pads, lots of ointments, witch hazel, vaporizers, crutches, and enema bags. He had twenty-seven cures for acid indigestion. He did carry magazines, and there was a glass case of cosmetics, but these were kept in moderation. This was, after all, a drugstore.

And if that truth needed a monument, he thought—

if someone doubted what Doc Garren stood for—Beauty!
Dedication! The things that last! Things worthwhile!—then
it was there, along the whole north wall, enshrined in the
antique soda fountain.

Its great mahogany mirror and high marble counter
were the first thing he'd seen when he came in the door
with the real-estate broker who cinched the deal. That
and the light—the afternoon light pouring in on it like oil,
deepening the grain of wood and stone, and somehow, he
thought, bringing out the best in him too. Later Doc added
the collection of huge apothecary jars in the window—like
stained-glass sculptures they were, like something holy.

Miss North Haven of 1938, then a senior at North
Haven Memorial High School (there were eight of them in the
class that year)—yes, the young Homecoming Queen herself
worked behind the soda fountain, bending gracefully to scoop
French vanilla onto sugar cones, five cents a dip. And she
would graciously make you cherry cokes, or lemon cokes, or
grape cokes if you wanted. Nothing was too much trouble—a
chocolate soda with chocolate ice cream? A coffee parfait with
butterscotch sauce and real whipped cream? Of course!

He had watched the light in her auburn hair, watched
it flash color as rich and deep as the mahogany behind
her—only richer and deeper and, god, how he loved her! So
much so that he never got over the joy that he felt when she
said yes, she would marry him, only first she would finish
high school. And he waited there in Garren's Drugstore,
measuring powders, funneling liquids, checking prescriptions
and checking again—he was so careful, even in those days,
when he saw the color of her hair reflected in every tawny-
colored cough syrup, in every amber vial.

She died giving birth to a baby they said was really better off dying too.

But at least he had his drugstore and his work. All the caring he would have given had she lingered in her dying, all the tender solicitude he was robbed of by her going, all this he poured into his pharmacy and the people who came there. In his memories of those grieving years, as he pictured them in the drugstore (and always his memories were framed in its front window), the glow of the apothecary jars was dulled by cloudy skies, from rainy days on rainy days.

In 1943, the St. Regis River overflowed. Polio hit town. People came in for headache powders, their faces haggard, asking his advice about braces—did he hear about the Kleins' little girl? Their eyes, looking into his, asked why this was happening to decent folks the likes of them, but truth was—he was more mystified than they were. He thought all of it—his wife's death, his firstborn's deformity, the town's blight, the nightmare of the world going to war—must be some terrible oversight that God would make good on, later when he noticed.

It hadn't occurred to him yet that some oversights can't be fixed. So in the meantime people handed their prescriptions up to him and, because he had to, Doc said "Can't rain forever."

He remarried. Linnie VanDusen was a rock-solid woman, gave him three sons with about as much trouble as a brood mare, kept his house clean, packed his lunches, and stayed away from the drugstore. It was a long, not unhappy marriage. In fact Doc was grateful to Linnie, and it bothered him when, standing near her rosewood casket with Father Burns, he'd found himself thinking of auburn hair.

Linnie took no part of him with her. A functional wife, she had never wanted to be more, and that to Doc's relief. Still she was dead. And so was McClusky. And he would be the first to say it was a shame.

⁂

"The usual, Doc," McClusky said, handing the amber bottle up for a refill.

⁂

McClusky had not been so fortunate in his choice for a wife. She spoke with a twang that grated on most folks' nerves and often came into the store for stomach remedies, complaining of gas. Sometimes McClusky had her get his prescription while she was in.

"Doc, I got such a pain," she said the last time Doc Garren remembered seeing her. She looked over her shoulder to see if their conversation was being overheard. She pressed the flats of her hands against her great belly, moaning, doubled over with pain. "Oh, god, my stomach's sore, I'm belchin'—'scuse me, Doc—I'm belchin' something awful. You suppose it's appendicitis?"

"No, no," said Doc, 'I'm sure it's nothing so serious. You've just been blessed with a bad digestion. You've got to cut out the cabbage, Mrs. McClusky. Here, this is something new you might try."

She took the bottle he offered, passing him McClusky's prescription vial. "My husband sent this along," she said. "He'd a brought it down hisself if he wudn't so hung over."

She shook her head. "And here I am, running his errands for him, and me gettin' an ulcer, no doubt. You think that man's got any consideration? You think he thinks about me the way I think about him? And worry about him?"

The pills were ready. She took the plastic tube from Doc's hand and said: "And this! If he don't watch it, he's gonna drop over dead one of these days." Her earnestness stopped just this side of wishful thinking.

And then, funny thing, he did drop over dead not two months later.

Doctor Cowley, who signed McClusky's death certificate, stopped by on his way home just before closing to have a chocolate soda with cherry ice cream, saying that Mrs. McClusky had been half-looped, was blubbering like a baby when he left. There must have been a big fight from the looks of the place, furniture overturned, a plate smashed. McClusky had died with both hands stiffened into fists.

Old Doc Garren was accustomed to people dying—certainly as used to it as the good doctor here slurping his soda at the marble counter in front of him. He was surprised at McClusky's passing and said so.

"Awful thing. He was just in here yesterday morning for his prescription and looked fine," he said, sponging down the counter. "Slossen's Grocery will be hard put to fill his shoes on the bowling team, I'd say."

"Maybe so," said Cowley, "but they're likely the only ones will miss him much."

"Who? McClusky?"

"Mean streak this wide," said the doctor, holding his hands either side of his soda glass. He tossed the spoon into it then, signaling he was finished. "Have to have an autopsy, of course. Something curious about the way he just keeled over. And his skin was mottled purple in places. Very odd."

Doc Garren couldn't help it. Unbidden, the memory came: McClusky saying "The usual, Doc." And his fingers, dense as hardwood, bumping up against Doc's own, while he handed him the bottle still warm from his hand—and now, thought the druggist, those hands were stiff and already losing substance, warmth being the first thing to go. Warmth being the last Doc knew of McClusky.

In Nortonville, the next town over, Doc's eldest son, Albert, had a funeral parlor. This bothered Garren though he never said so. It was just the thought of Albert handling stiffened people like McClusky, imagining him feeling people's bodies, and them unable to protest—no, no, they were dead—of course he knew that—and as his son said, somebody had to do it! But still this seemed to Doc a dire encroachment, a most ungracious trespass. Truth was, he was relieved that Albert rarely called, as he did the day after McClusky's passing.

Albert's voice had such a practiced stealth, that reciting a grocery list he still might sound as if he were revealing things unspeakable. And that is why Doc wasn't sure whether the hairs on his arm were standing up on end because of how his son was saying it, or whether he was reacting to something in his memory—just a flash—white pills tumbling from his hand.

"You musta known this guy McClusky. The Herald had him in the paper just last week. Bowled 265 in the tournaments."

"A course I know him. Sad thing."

The purplish mottles scattered like hibiscus on McClusky's milk-white body turned out to be his blood's doing. Thinned to the point that it slipped right past his capillaries, flooding into cells like the St. Regis River had swamped the North Haven lowlands back in '43, McClusky's blood had, so to speak, drowned him. Cowley's autopsy revealed Turgidaphene in his cells, left behind like debris left in the mud when the floodwaters fall back. Albert said he was a mess but McClusky would be his masterpiece. He would fix him up to look like natural. The Mrs. was taking it hard.

When he hung up the phone, Doc walked up the two steps to where his pharmacy was elevated in the back of the drugstore, smoothing the goosebumps on his arms—cold in here. Whistling, he began to check the stock on his shelves, straighten bottles, check and recheck. White pills kept tumbling into his memory, down the paper chute. McClusky's beefy hand, the same that once bowled eight straight spares, reached toward him.

Doc Garren checked his inventory, corroborated it with chit-sheets, marked it, counted it, then counted it again. A rare thing, he began to feel ill; even rarer, decided to close the drugstore a little early. Before he left, he folded the awning up like bats' wings against the outside wall.

At 8:00 A.M. Doctor Cowley called him at home, inquiring about the prescription Garren had mentioned filling for McClusky. When had it been?

"Thursday morning. Why you asking?"

"Just checking. Routine for the med report. Nice weekend coming up, looks like."

Doc hung up the phone, picked it up again, called Miss Reinhardt to ask could she unlock at nine? After lunch he was feeling well enough to go in for a while at least, and driving north into town he passed the new Walgreen's, as he did every morning, its front window plastered with posters for a vitamin sale.

There, entering the front door, was Mrs. McClusky. With one hand flat against her belly, she was pushing the plate glass door open with her free hand, her face looking pained. On an impulse Doc Garren turned into the Walgreen parking lot.

Walking across the blacktop, he was tempted to feel envious, thought what an advantage this corner lot was, and suspected the ease of parking was costing him business. When he pushed the door open, he heard no bell overhead, and felt a loss.

The ceiling of the new building was low and translucent, evenly lighted by fluorescent fixtures hidden behind plastic panels. Its blue-gray light stole color out of faces, but highlighted brightly packaged goods on all the shelves. Above them huge blue signs with white letters two feet tall, backlit with more fluorescent lights, guided you to where you wanted to go:

HEALTH AIDs—COSMETICS—HOUSEWARES—GIFTs—JEWELRY. Doc Garren walked down the aisles looking at bright orange signs taped on all the shelves: MAGIC FERN SHAMPOO HALF PRICE 12 OUNCES ONLY $1.59 GET AN EXTRA 3 OUNCES FREE NO CHARGE TWO

FOR ONE SALE FREE DISPOSABLE RAZOR WITH EVERY
PURCHASE THIS WEEK ONLY.

The shelves were loaded way up over his head—he
had to tilt back to see it all. Chrome glistened everywhere,
and everything such a buy! BUY NOW! SAVE NOW! OFFER
GOOD THIS WEEK ONLY! He felt relieved to finally see the
PHARMACY sign lighting up the end of an aisle straight
ahead of him. He was curious now, curious to see who
worked in this dead blue light.

A young man with blond hair and a white smock
stood behind an elevated counter, a foot-high wall of ribbed
glass separating him from the people down below, who were
clustered at the one opening in the wall, resembling a teller's
window. The young man looked bored. His eyes, when he took
the prescriptions handed to him, looked over people's heads
to a far corner of the drugstore and beyond. HI! MY NAME'S
MARK MORRIS, the orange letters of his nametag said.

Mark Morris had a computerized register that made
ripping sounds whenever he rang up a sale. Doc noticed
a large sign to one side of him that listed THEIR PRICE
vs. OUR PRICE and he stood there noting the names and
their prices—Amoxicillin, Quibron, Turgidaphene—until
suddenly he realized with a start that THEIRS was talking
about Garren's Drugstore and OURS (always less, even if
by only a few cents) meant the Walgreen's. This struck him
as a gossipy way to do business, really, discourteous to the
extreme! He was about to step forward, say, young man, I beg
your pardon—when he saw what he'd forgotten for a moment:
Mrs. McClusky.

She was standing with her arms crossed over her
belly, her feet planted far apart to support her weight, her

knees knocked together to form a buttress. As Doc moved toward her, one hand reaching out, he was thinking of a pink lotion he had bottled at the store that coated the stomach and soothed better than Pepto-Bismol. It would do her worlds of good....

She saw him out of the corner of her eye, jumped back as if she feared for her life. "Why ain't somebody arrested you yet?" she said.

Doc Garren looked around him to see who she was talking to—he must have missed something—but, no, she was talking to him.

"The savior of North Haven," she said next. "Does everybody so much good, always ready to lend a helpin' hand—god save 'em! You old coot! Folks been saying you're behind the times and my McClusky had to go and prove how much. I used to tell him you was senile, there oughta be a law against you pushin' pills, but, no, he liked the old-timey stuff, he told me. He wouldn't never listen to me—" Here she started to cry. "And now look where he is—"

Doc pulled out a handkerchief and handed it to her, waiting for the floor underneath him to stop weaving. "You just as good as poisoned him," she said, sobbing into the wadded cloth. "Folks just don't know how much I loved him." She turned again to Doc. "You're gonna pay for this," she said. "I'm gonna have your hide up on the door, I'm gonna have your license. You want to talk to me anymore? You talk to my lawyer!" With this she turned to face toward the pharmacy, crumbling Doc's handkerchief in her fist.

Meanwhile the young pharmacist had become aware of a drama going on in the group clustered below him. He dealt with it in the way he must have been taught at pharmacy school: "May I help you, madam?" he asked Mrs. McClusky.

"Ain't nobody can help me. Ain't nobody can raise the dead but Jesus."

Mark Morris turned to Doc Garren then: "May I help *you, sir?*"

For the next three days a fever weighted Doc's remembrances into oppressions too solid for this life, bearing down on his brain with incredible pressure: He watched McClusky's hand dissolve to bone when he bumped Doc's fingers reaching up for Turgidaphene, the flesh melting away like tallow, the flesh melting away. And little white pills, heavy as bullets, poured out of his great amber bottle, and poured and poured, filling up the backroom, giving off electric fumes that crackled in his nose, and poisoned him and everyone who came in through the door. Their bodies thatched the floor, laid this way and that, an arm extended out, a foot tripping another corpse, two heads intimate in death, one man frozen while laughing.

He was enough himself when he recovered to know that these were only nightmares, and nothing to be compared with the letter he got from the state licensing board. They had received complaint, they wrote him. They would review the case carefully.

Still, in the backroom, checking inventory, noticing with what ease one might accidentally—while listening to the bell out front perhaps, or catching a gleam of prism from the beveled mirror in the corner of your eye—

That is to say, how easy it might be to pick up the bottle of 100 mgs. Turgidaphene used in much more serious cases, instead of the 10 mgs. McClusky needed. Only a moment's inattention, one brief reverie someplace else, to come back unwitting to the unspeakable.

He had time now to think about such things, rattling around the store, much in solitude these days because business had dropped off some. Had dropped off quite a bit actually—you couldn't keep a thing like this quiet.

He pieced his memories together carefully, and little by little discovered a pattern. It seemed that life had always been waiting for him in ambush, now that he thought about it—and for others too. He began to picture all of North Haven walking about on rotted ice that heaved from their weight, giving premonition of the moment that some people would break through too quickly to stop themselves from falling into waters black and biting. And here was the awful thing, he thought—none of us having anywhere else to walk.

Part of him wanted to curse at the folks who said, "Good morning" as he stood there on the sidewalk, cranking the awning down—wanted to curse them for their politeness while they took their business to Walgreen's; but the other part of him was honest and couldn't blame them. And if not these folks, whom should he blame? The hardwood floors of the drugstore, warped and rolling from so many summers' heat and winters' frost, seemed sometimes to be moving under his feet.

Fool, he had thought himself safe within the drugstore. More than that, he had thought of Garren's Drugstore as a place where others could find safety as well, and him a lighthouse searching out remedies along the way to make it better. Now he saw things differently.

He remembered the time Mrs. Wright's brother-in-law got into his car to leave, both he and Mrs. Wright intent on the plumbing he had just fixed as a favor to his brother, Vince—both of them, mother and uncle, forgetting his nephew, who wasn't quite right and was scooping cinders with a tablespoon near the back tire of the Oldsmobile. All of them too busy to notice how one moment's inattention could crush the life out of someone.

And the time Titus Whitmore (with his gout no longer a bother, thanks to the prescription he got at Garren's) returned from the mailbox in a snowstorm, probably the hundredth he had lived through, to find that he had locked himself out. And climbing up on a windowsill to pry the window open, he fell and knocked himself out, the cold eating him alive for his mistake.

And what about his own Miss North Haven, the best trick life had played on him up to now, her alabaster skin unmarked by freckles—even now he remembered her shining bluish in the moonlight—perfect in everything she was, close to holy. Except for the half-being she birthed the night she died.

Not that life was all dirty tricks. There were other memories, happy ones. It was just that he could see now that their circumstances too were accidental. He had solved life's mystery and it was simple: Patterns sometimes fell into lucky formations. That was no reason to expect it to keep on.

He was determined to take this wisdom with him everywhere now. He knew people were saying he was breaking under the terrible guilt, talking to himself when no one was listening any more, making sense only half the time. But it wasn't that he was breaking so much—oh no, it was the icy ground underneath him that had broken, cleaving deeper holes you couldn't see. And he was warning them, warning, it could happen to them.

The boys on Slossen's team looked uncomfortable when he came to sit at their backs, munching peanuts while he watched the alley. They said "Hi Doc," but whatever else they said was out of earshot just between them—no one asked him what was good for earaches or the grippe. He knew they'd heard rumors Mrs. McClusky was suing him—you couldn't keep a thing like that quiet. But at the same time, he thought sure it was only a matter of explaining himself.

When a pinsetter didn't spit back Stu Prentice's ball, Doc said he wasn't surprised. All you had to do was take your eyes off the alley for just one second—to glance at a girl, to wave hi to a friend—just one second and you could kiss your new Brunswick goodbye and then how would you finish the game? Yessir, it'd happened to him more than once.

The boys on Slossen's team looked at him, their mouths slightly open—like a school of bass they were, nodding at him in unison.

Well, it was true just the same—take your eyes off what you should be looking at just for one moment and whole worlds were likely to pass away. What he felt was unfair about the whole thing was the not knowing, until he'd looked away, until that moment was past retrieving, what it was that was so important about that one moment. How could you tell—when one moment was strung with so many others, all of them seeming familiar and harmless, a string of pearly memories like any necklace of previous moments—that this one, this one, would be so important?

He tried to explain this to Bob Mills, his lawyer and friend, who interrupted Doc's explanation with what he thought was good news: Yes, yes, it was unfair, no doubt about it. The State Board agreed, they wanted this kept quiet. Doc should really have retired by this time anyway. He had served a good many years, he had friends. To have this one incident blot that all out—no, no, they wouldn't have it.

McClusky's wife would settle for three, maybe four thousand (that's the way it is with the ones who scream the loudest), and Prentice at the Herald was looking the other way on this one—decent man. Anyway, now Doc could retire, sell the store. "It is time," Mills said, putting an arm around Doc's shoulder while he walked him to the office door, "to take it easy, after all."

At that moment Doc looked down to see his friend walking over a wrought-iron floor register patterned like a gate there on the floor, like a gate—"Be careful!" Doc yelled, pushing Bob out of danger up against the wall with a jolt. "Don't trust those things," he said, with his face close enough to the lawyer's that Bob couldn't miss a thing.

In the space of the next few moments, eyeball to eyeball, Doc realized he had somehow failed to make Bob understand the urgency of the matter: How things like floors can't necessarily be counted on to hold up underneath you. At a loss to explain himself, Doc only repeated his warning in a whisper, surer than ever that it must be said: "Be careful," he said, letting go of the lawyer's shirtfront.

"Yes, Doc, I will," said Bob finally, sidling away toward the door without taking his eyes off Doc. "I will," he said.

Doc sat in his store watching the light illuminate the giant jars of colored water, trying to think why his revelation kept eluding him whenever he tried to tell others. He was filled with memories of what had happened here and who had come here. He stopped to tell the strangers who came to his close-out sale (all of it arranged by his son Albert— well, somebody had to do it!) about Titus Whitmore and Becky Prentice and the year of the flood of 1943. Memories strung on a silvery line all connected now and exact in their significance and their triviality.

Or so it seemed. But he kept telling it, hoping that in listening to himself he might pick up what he had missed somehow: clues to explain what had happened to him. Newcomers he didn't recognize—looking for bargains and nothing more, trying to outsmart fate without paying full price—backed toward the door, with their arms filled, nodding, yes, yes, thank you very much, and to themselves— What a crazy old man!

They weren't interested in his passing. Garren knew it. But that really didn't seem to matter now. He was thinking so hard these days, remembering, it was like he was under water. That was it, the terrible pressure: He had fallen through the rotten ice and, instead of black water, he had found it fantastically colored and beyond his knowing.

There McClusky's hand floated toward him asking for the usual. And a school of bass, their mouths open like the boys on Slossen's team, nodded in unison when he burbled what was coming to him with the water pressing him down, filling his ears with wonderful garbled explanations.

But whenever his head broke the surface of the water—when he found himself back in Garren's Drugstore, just sitting there at the soda fountain, with the light from the mirror's edge dancing on the counter there next to his hand—red, blue, yellow—he could never remember what the explanation had been, and he wanted desperately to know it.

CARPOOL

I swear I would have heard the alarm, except I was standing on the beach with Aunt Caroline who's been dead for two years. What a nightmare, my favorite aunt! She was dressed in purple knickers and these glittery stockings, all of which seemed perfectly normal. And there was this big, white yacht coming toward the two of us, going faster and faster the closer it came. Me, I wanted to run, but someone on deck pointed a flood light on us, and Aunt Caroline said, "Smile, dear. They're making a documentary," and that yacht, it kept right on coming, right up over the sand; and clean as a knifeblade, it sliced my aunt into two pieces, only she kept on smiling, subdivided now, and that light kept on burning, so bright I could see it, reddish-orange, through my eyelids; and all of a sudden, I was under water, and I heard these burbling noises and my eyes were closed and I pulled myself up on handfuls of water, gasping for air, afraid I wouldn't make it—

Honest to god. I was sure I wouldn't make it.

It takes a nearly drowned person a few minutes to come to—I mean I couldn't figure out where I was at first.

I blinked up into this light, and then I saw a young man standing in this doorway with his hand on a light switch. And for a moment—not long—I wondered who he was and why he looked so angry. And then I remembered. This was my son, and I glanced at the clock and understood the scowl on his face.

"We're late again," Brian, who was sixteen, said, but I was already flinging back the covers, screaming, "Oh, no, we're late again! Come on, hurry up."

I ran into the kitchen to put on coffee and toast, then back to my bedroom to throw on my clothes. When the kettle began whistling, I came back to find the toast popped up and cold. Brian and I ate it with the margarine waxy on top, neither one of us speaking, at opposite ends of the table. After that, we both squeezed into the bathroom, me leaning over the sink putting on my mascara, he glaring at me in the mirror, a toothbrush jammed into his mouth.

Then I couldn't find my shoes, my only decent heels. Brian had his jacket on by that time and was standing by the back door, his books piled in his arms. "I'm going out to the car," he said and slammed the door behind him.

I tore through my bedroom, looking everywhere. Brian's third grade picture was there on my dresser-top; he beamed down on me through two missing teeth. I tried to think of what his smile looked like now that all his big teeth are in, but I couldn't remember, he's been scowling so long. Finally I saw the toes of my shoes sticking out from under the bed. I rushed to put them on, hopping over to the kitchen door on one foot while I pulled the strap over my heel. I cut the corner too short, though, and skidded into the refrigerator, knocking my lunchbag with an over-ripe peach inside, splat, onto the floor.

On my way out of the driveway, I almost backed into a station wagon.

Brian said, "Ma-ohm," like that: two syllables, the last one going down low, "Ma-ohm, watch out, will you? Geez."

I pretended I hardly noticed—screech of tires, the angry roar of the station wagon zooming around our rear end. I reached over and turned on the radio, which is something Brian always does, but this morning I wanted to beat him to something, even if Larry Lavinia is the last thing I wanted to hear. Lavinia was just finishing up his showbiz report, which meant it was quarter-to. My carpool leaves at quarter-to. That was something else against me; no bag phone.

❦

I got hung up behind a truck. I'd been reading this book on positive thinking, which is something I am trying to develop to keep my sanity these days, and it occurred to me that if I just looked on the bright side, this slow ride was actually giving me a few extra minutes with my son, which was something I needed.

I've been worried about our hardly talking anymore. Brian did not want to choose parental sides in the divorce, so he compromised by washing his hands of both of us. He was still living with me, for convenience. I'd see him on his way to his bedroom, at the kitchen desk with a telephone attached to his head, while he ate, or if I was lucky, in the car. But I keep telling myself, it's the quality of time spent with your kids that counts, not the quantity.

"So, Brian," I said to him. "How's your life been going lately?"

"Okay," he said, and then right away, "Hey, REO Speedwagon." He reached over to turn the volume up on the radio, looked up at the ceiling, his head bobbing. "Take it on the run, baby, that's the way you wahn-na, baby...."

We finally made it to Tony Marcheli's, Brian's best friend and a smart-ass. All right, the kid had real smarts, too, and initiative, a job. An intact family. Tony also had his driver's license and a '65 Chevrolet he's repainted himself. Every morning I'd drop Brian off and he and Tony would go to school in style.

"Have a good day," I said to Brian, like I always do.

"See ya," he said, opening the door. He got out without so much as looking at me, like he always does, and walked around the front of the car. Just as he was smack in front of the hood, I tooted the horn to make him jump. I wanted to make him laugh. But he kept on walking like he hadn't heard it, just because he did not want to give me the satisfaction. Stubborn kid. One of these days I am going to have a diesel horn installed and blast him right off the street.

I drove three more blocks to the parking lot where I meet Barbara and Louanne. I didn't expect to see them still waiting there, but one of them must have been late, too. There they were, both in Barbara's car, a plume of white exhaust curling around the tires.

I pulled up next to them, jamming my brakes so hard the car rocked a little as it stopped, then grabbed my stuff and walked over to them. I had to balance my brown-bag lunch and some file folders, my high heels poking holes in the gravel for a very unsteady trip—especially since I was trying not to get peach juice on anything.

The air inside the car was warm and plastic-smelling, different from the cool morning air. I slid into the back seat, said "Good morning. I'm sorry I'm late."

"Good-morning-good-morning," the two women answered.

Seatbelt fastened, belongings arranged on the seat next to me. Then the smooth take-off of Barbara's Grand Prix pressing me gently into the velour cushions of the seat. We drove in silence to the interstate, inwardly changing gears ourselves, relieved to have arrived at one place and be on our way to another.

Louanne was looking out the window at the side traffic rushing by as we merged into it. Finally, she said, "There's frost in the fields this morning. It's supposed to stay cool today."

Louanne gives us the weather report every morning. The weather is very important to her. It matters to her if it rains or it doesn't, if the frost is a killing one, or the wind changes direction. Louanne is nearly six feet tall and lives in the country, has never married and still calls all women "ladies." Whenever she has to go from her department to someplace else in the office, she walks with her shoulders hunched over, eyes cast down, trying not to be noticed. She has just the opposite effect. She'd be amazed to know that everyone knows who she is, or that she brought us an hilarious moment when she sent the whole office a postcard from San Francisco that read: "Didn't visit Chinatown, but went to Burger King for lunch where Chinese people waited on us."

Louanne belongs to a fundamentalist church, which may explain her strange combination of timidity, humility and a rockbed sense of superiority. I've seen these traits at odds in her face when she's made some self-righteous pronouncement; you can see she's scared to death to be doing it, but proud of herself, too.

Once driving home—I don't remember why—I told Louanne and Barbara about a longtime family friend, a man named Otto Clemmons. The first blow had come when poor Otto's only son got into serious trouble with the law. And then, just when he began to think about retirement, he lost his job, his pension, and finally any inkling of why he was bothering with anything. Otto went off to the garage one night, saying he was driving down to the drugstore. Only he sat in the car with the motor running until Mary, his wife, wondered what on earth was taking him so long. She found him with the garage door still shut, and Otto gone much further than she could have imagined.

Louanne listened to all this and I could see she was just waiting for me to finish—fluttering her eyelids, composing her expression to fit the importance of what she'd expound. She waited a moment to be polite. And then she said, "According to the Christian faith, suicide is a sin." Her lips were drawn back in a quivery smile. Why was she smiling, I wondered. What could be funny?

Most of the time I feel sorry for Louanne, but after that, it was days before the urge to kill her left me, and even longer before I could speak to her without clenching my teeth. I finally figured out the reason it bothered me so much—aside from the fact that it was a mean way to sum up Otto's life. That half-smile got me.

Daniel, my ex, had smiled like that; such a reasonable gargoyle. "Look," he said to me in his calm, measured voice, 'It's just not working...." Only his mouth was fighting it, like Louanne's, snagged at the corners by pretense, lips trembling, wanting to scream out his judgment, as he did later on. Right then he wanted to be the nice guy, so I'd say, of course, go on your own way with my blessing. After all, you've been such a swell guy.

The hypocrite. Christ, I liked him better when he yelled.

"I'm going to need to drive in by myself tomorrow," Barbara was saying. "John has a dentist appointment, and I'll have to leave work early. One of you will have to drive."

Louanne, in the passenger seat, half turned toward me, opened her mouth, hesitated, and then went ahead: "I can drive tomorrow, Alice, if it's all right with you. Unless you want to drive. Or maybe you have something planned and you'd rather drive. But if you want...." Her eyelids fluttered and she glanced at me, then away.

"Okay," I answered. "I'll drive Friday then, and next week it's my turn to drive three days."

Barbara nodded approval at this plan. Then Louanne turned all the way around toward me and looked especially earnest. "You should really have your tires checked," she said. "I noticed they looked low this morning, Alice. They say you should have them checked once a month." Her eyelids began to flutter—timidity beginning to win out— then she looked down. "It'll ride better, too," she said, though I could barely hear her, and then she turned back around.

I felt absolutely no obligations to respond or even to acknowledge her. I had seen other people dismiss her like that. She seemed not to expect anything else. And for a moment I thought how sad that was, but not for long.

The Grand Prix cut a swath through the morning fog, its motor nearly silent, passing other cars without effort. It is a rich maroon color inside and out, and everything including the digital clock and the rear window defogger, works correctly. This seems the appropriate car for Barbara because everything in her life looks to me like it works correctly. Her husband makes a lot of money and enjoys tinkering around the house. He just built a wooden deck off their living room and next he plans to install a sliding glass door. He is prematurely gray and quite handsome, with a slight pot that gives him a safe, married look. Barbara has never said so, but I am willing to bet just from looking at their son, John, that he has no smart-ass friends.

✍

We were driving under the bridge at Union Street. I've never told Barbara and Louanne, as often as we've gone by this spot, but it's where I lived when I first got married. Eighteen years ago, a shingled house with shutters, a young man my parents said had great promise. And then he says, hiding blame behind bared teeth, it's just not working. It wasn't working all right, none of it was: the great promise, the high expectations, him—he wasn't working.

He used to say to me, "If you'd only give me the emotional support, if you didn't ask so much. If you didn't expect for me to always carry you, my God, when is it my turn to be carried?" And then he got himself fired again, and his mother sent money again, and he sat at home watching game shows on TV, thinking deep thought, too deep for me, surely. And when I came home from work he turned his head so my lips just grazed his jawbone, stubble scratching my mouth. The man who had great promise. The man who broke great promises. The man, broken.

I left him finally. Even the divorce had to be my job. It had to look like my fault, you see, and I must have done it well because Brian thought so, and my mother in-law thought so. And my parents were careful to explain that when it came to such things, I had to make my own decisions and not involve them. Which meant they thought it was my fault, too.

None seemed to blame him when he found a new woman two months after I'd gone. I wouldn't doubt he made love to her in our bed, probably right under the Renoir print I bought us on our third anniversary. I couldn't bear to take it when I left; he always said he loved it.

I tried not to ask Brian questions about his father and the new girlfriend, but I couldn't seem to help myself. And when things seemed to be going so well for him, I couldn't stand it. It didn't seem right, not while I was going crazy.

So I learned to cope. I arranged to have no free time. I took night classes. I planned a career strategy, read Games Your Mother Never Taught You. And most of the time now, I'm okay. Last month, I got a promotion.

Last month I also found out that Daniel makes jokes to Brian all the time about how I'm doing so well, how I'm so much better off than he is. Brian told me this, not looking at me, just shaking parmesan cheese on his spaghetti and staring at it.

"So what dentist are you going to?" Louanne was saying to Barbara, and Barbara looked blank and said, "Dentist? What dentist?"

Louanne said, "The one you're taking your boy John to."

Barbara turned pink and looked embarrassed, said, "Oh, I forget—Dr. Johnson.

"Dr. Johnson?" said Louanne. "I don't know of any dentist by that name. Where is he from?"

"Oh? Danesville, I think."

"That's an awful long way to go for a dentist."

"Yes, well, he's good, and anyway, maybe his name isn't Johnson. I can't remember."

Louanne looked surprised. Barbara looked uncomfortable. She knew as well as I did that this is the sort of thing Louanne relishes taking time with, like the weather.

"You can't remember," she said. "Well, let me see. I think there's a Dr. Josephson in Danesville, but I always thought he was a foot doctor. Was it Josephson you were thinking of?"

"Maybe. Yes, probably, that's it." Barbara turned

to me, then, changing the subject. "Alice, would you like to come over for dinner tonight? Bill's new boss is coming over and I hear he's single."

I blushed and felt immediately appalled by how eager I felt. "Oh, I couldn't," I said.

"Oh, come on, a man his age, never been married? He's got to be used to that sort of thing." Barbara laughed and, not knowing what else to do, I joined in. He was gay, no doubt.

Meanwhile Louanne had been looking up at the ceiling of the car. Now she said, "Jackson maybe. Was it Jackson?"

"I don't know," Barbara said in an exasperated tone of voice. "On second thought," she said to me, "maybe we should wait and let me check him out first. I mean whenever I meet someone that old who's never been married, I wonder what on earth is wrong with him. Maybe he's got a third eye or something!" Barbara laughed again.

I noticed Louanne glance at her, but Barbara didn't see it, didn't even seem to realize what she'd just implied about Louanne's marital status. Me, I wondered what Barbara thought about divorced people, and found myself rubbing the skin between my eyes, feeling for something undetected.

Louanne got out a small notebook she keeps in her purse, and held it upright in one hand, writing so that no one could see what she wrote. What was she always writing in there, licking the tip of the pencil before she put it to paper? September 29, she'd start out. Then maybe something about the weather: Frost in fields. And notes to herself: Check Alice's tires. Dentist mystery. Johnson? Josephson? Jackson? Pray for Barbara. Suicide is a sin.

Louanne finished writing, flipped the notebook cover closed and tucked it away in her purse, sniffing once. Then she turned to look out the window and watch the fields. Barbara was still doing diversionary chatter. She didn't seem to notice Louanne staring out the window with a purpose.

I wondered what was really going on with Barbara's son, John. Maybe the dentist was a ruse. Maybe the kid was really a drug addict or a shoplifter and she had to take him to court or bail him out. Come to think of it, maybe John was a ruse. Maybe she wasn't really taking him anywhere. Maybe she was meeting a lover or a lawyer. Who knows, really, what lurks behind the thermal drapes of Barbara's living room? Or anyone's, for that matter.

On the other hand, maybe Barbara really just forgot where the dentist lived and what his name was. Didn't I misplace my own son's name just this morning? Who is this kid, I asked myself, staring at him when I first woke up from drowning. Didn't my mother always call me Robert-Mark-er-Alice, going all the way down through the order of her children's births before she came to me? Oh, it's you.

I looked out the window at all the cars shushing by, and it struck me how all of them were full of people—all these people I didn't know, and yet I felt like I knew them, felt like I knew all of us, wounded by our own knife-edged dreams. And we keep going. Some of us with bruises nearly healed, new dreams in sight, limping along in a rush to the next bashing. Some not so lucky, already close to keeling over. Some close to lying down.

So turn up the stereo and look out the window with Louanne. At roads that mark our comings and goings, their edges blurred by our speed; at people sealed up in cars.

I pressed my forehead against the glass of the window, feeling how cold it was, so cold it made my head ache after a moment. I saw myself honking the horn at Brian as he walked in front of my car, I saw him keep on walking.

Barbara flicked on the turn signal as we pulled off the exit ramp. We stopped at the stop sign behind three or four other cars and waited our turn. Pulling up and then stopping, pulling up and then stopping. River Street is normally crammed with traffic at this time, everyone rushing to work. It takes daring and a steely disregard for others to squeeze your way in. I sat watching the tailpipe of the car just ahead of us with its flicker of white exhaust, wondering how it must look to see that stuff, like angel hair, flattening out, seeping out, from under a garage door.

Suddenly, I heard the squeal of brakes from the direction of the intersection. I looked up and thought I could make out a figure running through the traffic, weaving in and out, but I couldn't tell exactly what was happening. A car had stopped in the middle of River Street. Horns began honking, several windows rolled down. The man in the car just ahead of us stuck his head out and began shouting at the guy ahead of him. "Go around!"

Then suddenly, the person I thought I saw at first materialized right in front of our line of cars. The car ahead of us, which had been crawling forward, swerved a little, and then jammed on its brakes. A boy in jeans, barefoot and shirtless, ran toward us down the road.

Barbara must've hit him because he pitched forward and sprawled onto the hood, his face suddenly huge in the windshield just in front of Louanne. She gasped and drew back. Barbara gave a short scream. I leaned forward to try to get a better look at him. And then he was gone.

I turned in my seat to watch him go, stunned by his expression for that moment, his mouth gaping open, like a drowning person, it seemed, or maybe he was trying to form a silent protest? We three must have looked so comfortable inside, dressed in our business suits, seated here on burgundy plush.

I could still make him out, staggering through traffic, barely missing disaster again and again. A squad car pulled up behind the line of cars. Two policemen got out and one of them, putting an arm around the boy's shoulder, eased him into the squad car, its flashing lights whirling. I turned back around in my seat to see Barbara patting her breastbone, panting, "Is he nuts? I nearly hit him. I think he wanted me to hit him."

Traffic began moving again. We eased out into River Street. I looked back to see the squad car pulling out into the lane of traffic next to us, passing us. We stared as they came alongside us, but all we could see was a small figure in the back seat, nothing unusual. They were in their car, we in ours, headed in the same direction.

JUNE ODET AND THE COUNTESS

The two sisters, trying hard to feel sisterly, sit with elbows on the table, soft drinks between them, trying to think of that woman's name, the neighbor from their childhood. They had called her the Countess when they were still girls, but she had a real name, too; both of them feel it on the tip of the tongue.

God, says Nancy, the younger by three years. She can see her yet... that arrogant head, that fine-boned jaw, face as oval as a cameo brooch. Can she really still be alive?

Incredible when so much else has changed, they are thinking. A shy silence comes between them then, a half-moment really, but seeming to go on and on, so that they both rush to fill the emptiness. Hadn't they just driven by her house in the rented car, and remarked on it—how the place hadn't changed a bit? White gingerbread porch, black shutters, and that signature of hers from summers long ago—coral geraniums set out on broad steps the color of turquoise.

The Chinese elm in front has grown huge and overarching. A surprise, seeing it again, and remembering an importance it seems impossible they could have forgotten. June Odet had been a permissive mother, but on this one subject, she was harsh, she was righteous, she was Elmer Gantry in a housedress. That tree might just as well have been planted in Eden, for breaking this one rule, climbing this elm, would make them guilty as Adam and Eve, she told them. "And you know who will be like the Wrath of God, don't you?"

Well, they did know at the time, and remembered what she'd said the moment they realized that Katherine—who was nine that year and showing off for Nance—was actually stuck there in the tree's forbidden branches. They had remembered and time slowed down even in the memory, their movements turned leaden, so that they halfway believed this must be the beginning of eternity, their growing panic at not knowing what to do next, surely the beginning of hell.

All that time, the Countess had watched them from behind a gauze curtain, her anger, cool and silent, radiating out to them. And now Katherine and Nancy try to remember that woman's name—though really it is a way of looking at their mother out of one corner of the eye, so to speak, not straight on, not full into her lost, homely face.

Nance, the braver of the two, and having learned from their mother to laugh at things to whittle them down to size, does at least dare to talk about how she ran to fetch her mother from her canning that day, and how mother June had looked that day: climbing the elm with her print apron still on, red-faced, embarrassed, and so puffing angry that Nance could see poor Kathy hadn't known whether to be more afraid of being stuck there or of being rescued. From below, Nance had been mortified to catch a glimpse of her mother's great white, cotton drawers, out in plain view on a public street.

The two sisters, nearing 40 now, are at the Howard Johnson's just outside North Haven. There is just one other car in the gravel parking lot besides their rented one; all the traffic takes the Interstate now, three miles east of Lake Michigan, the little town abandoned to fruit farms there on the sandy bluff.

Howard Johnson's had the good sense to get out; the man who bought it has renamed it The Family Inn, but kept the orange roof, the captain's chairs. He has dark rings under his eyes and has not shaven, yet is courtly when he recognizes Nancy's last name on the register. Their mother has been on the radio, is known in this town, and these women with their short, stocky builds do look like her, though one of them is fashionably dressed. He says, as he hands them their menus, "I was sorry to hear about June."

They thank him kindly, but neither woman takes up the name he drops. June is their mother's middle name, taken up when she went public. The sisters sit on turquoise vinyl, Kathy stirring her soda with a straw, rushing the ice around and around inside the glass. There is a crack in the thermo-pane window next to her, its corner filled with milky condensation; it's cold outside.

The woman whose name they are trying to remember is Sylva Van Zant; later Nance will remember it without effort, lying in bed as she stares at the moon through a sliver where the drapes don't quite reach the edge of the motel window—Sylva Van Zant, the syllables will roll up from some silenced space with a sense of relief, but also of wonderment. For why is she thinking of her now, of all times, just as she is recognizing how often her mother must have been afraid, how frequently brave? The man on the moon mirrors the question; his grief howls what she cannot.

But now Nance, watching Katherine swirl her ice, is trying to remember that woman they both had loved to hate, while she is, in fact, avoiding talking about their mother's death. At the same time she is wishing that Katherine, the elder, would just go ahead and begin it, the hated, the necessary talk.

Rheba June Odet had been a lover of country music and cotton dresses, of people who just dropped in, cultivator of numberless avocado plants on every window sill in the house. Grown from huge split seeds, they were—and free! she used to say—an extra, compelling bonus for her, the way she measured everything that was Best in Life; never mind free was all she could afford.

June spoke like that, in homilies—The Best Things in Life Are Free. Nothing Ventured, Nothing Gained. Little Strokes Fell Great Oaks—and ingenuously, as if she'd just heard this news a minute ago, answering a knock at the front door from the Muses.

Nothing Ventured—she said, standing in a pile of broken-up plaster, tearing out the attic walls to enlarge Katherine's tiny bedroom upstairs, a job that she never quite finished. Nothing Ventured—she said, clipping out stories of big city crimes—Strangler on the Loose, Why You're More Likely to Be Killed in an American City—while she urged her girls onward toward adventure.

"Know what you're up against," she said, handing the clippings to Nance who was college bound that year and dreaming of New York galleries. "But you go, Nancy Mae. Go with your eyes open. Nothing Ventured, Nothing—Gained"—their mother said, gasping on the phone for breath, calling from the Pine Wood Nursing Home where they'd installed her over protest. It was time she get back on her feet, she said. She had tried this rest business, hadn't she? Enough Was Enough.

Lung cancer, and June, too easy-going to stop her smoking right up to the end. Jaunty phone calls to her daughters, all undone by deep, dry gasps that sheared off talk. Little Strokes Fell Great—

Katherine and Nancy, a thousand miles apart, reconnected by the phone call each got from the Pine Wood Nursing Home's Executive Director, crackling a message in snapping and static, unattached to anything they could possibly picture. It was hard to trust this blind voice, these rumors—their mother suddenly worse; their mother dead.

Now Kathy sucks the last bit of color from the ice. "I suppose we had better see about our room," she says. "I should give Hal a call." She begins rummaging through her purse. "And to think, we can come back here for our dinner. And our breakfast."

Nancy nods, looking around the place; only she sees, not the restaurant, but a memory: Rheba June Odet flipping pancakes in mid-afternoon. As usual, answering desire over duty. Both she and Nancy know that Nance is skipping school, not really sick.

There is a crack in the window over the sink, and Nance, swinging one foot crazily as she sits with elbows on the table, smelling the hot metal smells and the butter, imagines that the steam-filled window with its sill lined with glasses of avocado starters is really a fish tank, something she wants very badly. She makes a fish face by pooching her lips together and blowing out her cheeks, and her mother, laughing at her with a cigarette in the corner of her mouth, bends close and gives her the first, the choicest, pancake.

Out loud Nance says, "It's too bad Ma couldn't hold onto the house." Her mother's pond was empty of water now. It had crabgrass growing in the cracks.

"And have all that to worry about, too? Those piles of hers? All those Avon bottles?" Kathy takes out three bills and lays them on the table, and Nance recalls that her sister had always had perfect school attendance. "No," Kathy says. "Bad as this is, it's better everything's gone already and taken care of. You ready?"

Kathy takes charge because she is the older of the two of them and, Nance believes, the more talented, the more promising. By most standards she's done very well. She married the president of a small manufacturing company in Evanston and has a beautiful house, expensive clothes. Yet they have hit hard times, she has said. It seems odd to Nance, who has on shoes that are clunky and dated, that Kathy can talk about being poor, dressed in an expensive tweed suit, pulling on cream-colored kid gloves.

Earlier she told Nance, "I've had to give up my painting classes."

"You can't do that! You loved them, they were making you happy!"

Her deprivation makes Nancy feel guilty. It is Katherine who came up with the plane tickets for both of them, though Hal and Marilyn, her step-daughter, had to stay behind. "There's no way you and I won't be there, at least," she promised Nancy, bolstering her up, unasked, for being broke again. "We owe Ma that much, poor old gal."

Nance remembers cringing, phone next to her ear, as

she pictured her mother's face listening to herself described that way. She would have taken a deep drag on her cigarette, exhaled through her nose in two plumy streams, unblinking, as she assessed the daughter who had just said that. The one who adds streaks to her dark hair. Wears silk scarves to camouflage a too-sturdy neck. In her mind, Nance watches their mother take the butt and twist it flat in an ashtray.

Nancy says now, reaching for her purse, "Let me pay for this at least." But Katherine waves the thought away with a gloved hand. She won't hear of it.

Later that afternoon they go to the Van Dusen Funeral Home over in Nortonville to make arrangements, because they do cremations. Kathy admires a beige metal casket, elegant with pearl columns at each corner, but Nancy reminds her that their mother had wanted no fuss.

Al Garren, once a jock senior when Kathy first entered high school, is now the Funeral Director. Like an elderly uncle, he guides them through the process, cupping his hand under one or the other's elbow for steerage. Odd, how intelligent his face seems now that his hair is gone, Nance thinks. Her senses are tight-wound, keyed up to receive distractions wherever she can find them.

Katherine is all business. Efficient but thorough, she considers each step carefully, pausing finally just before putting pen to contract. She comments with a single sniff, "I guess Mother's wanting to spare us expense was just her wishful thinking."

Albert blushes a little but keeps his hands folded together in his lap, sacrosanct. "As I said, there are regulations about cremation, Katherine."

'Nancy, maybe we should have a regular funeral at

this cost. I hate to see us spend this much and get so little," says Kathy.

"That would be Burial with Viewing and Attendance," Albert indicates on the form between them, "rather than Immediate Cremation."

Nance pretends to be looking out the window at something. Her mother would have been outraged that the funeral home was fleecing them at a time like this. She might have called up the radio talk show, as she used to when she was outraged about some injustice, which happened regularly.

Nance says nothing because she knows that Kathy remembers perfectly well what her mother wanted. Not to put on a show for people—to wind up good fertilizer, she'd said. That was a good, a holy aim, higher than a lot of church folks as far as she could tell.

"All right, Kathy," Nance says finally, when her sister still hesitates over the contract. "But money's the least of it, you know that."

⁂

Katherine and Nancy hold vigil at the Van Dusen Funeral Home, expecting no one, for who could be left? But a group of older women come in, fellow volunteers at the hospital auxiliary. They act as if they know Nancy and Katherine, and Nance thinks some of them do look vaguely familiar. She begins adlibbing, repeating names she hears them use. That's kind of you to say, Mrs. Miller. Mrs. Watts, how good of you to come.

Their standard comments—June Always Had a Smile

for Me, followed by My, Doesn't She Look Natural?—take
on a comforting rhythm. And since no one appears to be
embarrassed at saying the same nice things over and over
to them, Nance believes they are sincere, and in return
is sincerely glad they came. Still, she has an easier time
accepting a comment from an old man in a baggy, pinstripe
suit: June had her nose in everything, he says.

Then Vic Walton, the disk jockey at W-OSH, comes in
to pay his respects and tells them the history they all know—
how Rheba June called in so often during his show, asking
for country tunes, speaking her mind on this and that, that
he finally invited her to join him, as a DJ. And she had, by
god! Walked in the front door and took to the airwaves like a
duck to water.

Now the piped-in organ music ends and there is Vic
Walton's voice coming over the speakers, telling them about
a tire sale at Pacquin's Tire and Auto Parts, and then a click,
and there is June Odet's voice: "Voice of the People," she says,
"you're on the air."

Everyone in the place stops what they are in the
middle of saying. They look up at the ceiling, searching for
June Odet, public personality and the mother of Nancy and
Katherine. Katherine looks at her sister, aghast.

"That's her, that's your mother," Vic Walton says. Then
he raises his voice for the others: "It's her, folks. It's all right,
it's a tape; she wanted it played."

And with that the small crowd buzzes: For heaven's
sake, I never heard of such a ...did you ever? And here and
there a gentle note of laughter, made a little bolder each
time when someone else dares to laugh—Leave it to June—
Shhhh, listen.

Another woman's voice, sharper, arid, higher, begins screeching: "And I just wanted to say that farmers in these parts are between a rock and a hard place with those new OSHA laws and having to have bathrooms for every one of them migrants..."

"Mr. Walton," Katherine looks panicked. "I'm not sure we should allow this. I mean, people are here to pay their respects. This is just—"

"It's what she wanted," Vic Walton says, crossing his arms, cocking his head to indicate that he is trying to hear the tape and she should be quiet.

"Well, that may be, but I am the executor of her estate—"

Nance can hear her mother say, "Claire Dobson, we thank you for calling. We do enjoy it so when you call."

"—And those migrants, they don't even take care of nothin', they wreck everything in sight that's not nailed down—"

"Good bye now, Claire. Time's up." Click. "I do hate to hang up on people," June Odet is saying, "but now and again Claire just has more than her fair share of say—but we love you, Claire! There's another call. Voice of the People, You're on the air—"

Nance interjects herself, body and all, between Katherine and the disc jockey. "People seem to be enjoying it, Kath. I mean, it is typical. People know she was that way." And now even their memories would call her June.

Katherine sets her mouth, closes her eyes—"You would think that she could at least die with a little dignity," she says. "You would think that this, at least, could be something to remember with a sense of pride—"

People seem to enjoy themselves; they sway to the fiddles when the music is on, talk and laugh while they listen to radio star June Odet, same as when she was alive, just like they remember her.

For the sisters, the voice and the twang of guitars conjures up the odd combinations of color their mother would wear, the whoosh of the cushions whenever she dropped her weight into an arm chair all at once. Nance despises Katherine's squirming, but can't help but remember herself: the dark hair that had started to sprout on her mother's chin, the eyes waning smaller in the growing moon of her face, smaller and squinting from cigarette smoke.

Just that morning, Nance's stomach folded over at the sight of her mother's resemblance in the motel room's mirror. How could you help being your own mother's daughter? What real chance did you have?

Albert Garren comes up to report he hasn't had so many sign into the guest book since the Webster's little girl was killed by that hit-and-run driver, and Nance tamps down her feelings, manages to say for the both of them—Kathy still speechless—that they are very moved.

That night, in the motel room, staring at the moonlight along one edge of the drapes, Nance will think how ironic that Kathy and she—and June Odet herself— had themselves been so sorely disappointed, wanting June to be tidier and slimmer, put in order by the attention and money of men, not overtaken by small children and animals and too many plants and too many ideas, and too many appetites finally.

They had wanted her to be Sylva Van Zant, she will realize (and at that moment, the name will bubble up). In a white house with shutters and coral geraniums, an oval brooch at her throat. The wraith of Sylva, the ghost of what they should be, who drew them fast like a magnet and when the poles were upended, who repulsed them, too, in a rhythm of inhalation, exhalation, admired and scorned in equal parts.

June Odet had been prevented from teaching Sunday School in the Dutch Reform Church because Sylva Van Zant, whose husband was still alive in those days and a deacon, thought it improper for a divorced woman. In retaliation, their mother did not allow Katherine Louise or Nancy Mae to cut across the corner of the Van Zant lawn, nor to climb their elm tree.

All of which is why, when the Countess appears there at the door of the funeral home, Nance remembers all over again the weight of her presence, both real and imagined—though she still fails to name her.

The Countess walks through the vestry, declines to sign her name in the book and without speaking to anyone, comes to stand in front of Nance. Her handshake is the barest touch on the fingertips of Nance's extended hand. She says, "Your mother was dearer to me than you may have known. I listened to her on the radio," she says, dropping her arm. "The whole town listened to her, you know." Katherine comes closer. Nance can see that she is amazed to see her too, and that her sister is also failing to shake the name loose.

Fortunately, the woman seems to think no formalities are necessary. She says, "Your mother was what you call a real character, you realize."

Nance can feel herself bristling; the pole has just

reversed. The nerve! But the Countess quickly adds, "No, I mean that she was true to herself. Yes, a compliment, that's what I meant."

Kathy murmurs something to serve as a bowl for that offering, and Nance inclines her head in respect. Overhead they can all hear the voice of June Odet, announcing a tune, "On the Wings of a Snow White Dove."

Nance thinks, if only this woman knew the times she had been the subject of discussions at their dinner table. Now what do you think the Countess would do? her mother would ask, pursing her lips to mock her. They had envied her and hated her and now here she stood, on an errand to tie everything up with lace.

"Do you remember that time she caught you climbing my elm?"

"We were just talking about it this morning," says Katherine, relieved to have a civil subject. "We drove by your house and wondered how you were—didn't we, Nance? And talked about Mother climbing up the tree to rescue me, how ridiculous she must have looked—"

"I still laugh to think of it." The lips of the Countess draw back in what is clearly an unaccustomed motion, to smile briefly, and Nance catches a glimpse of badly fitted teeth. "I wanted to shout out at you not to be afraid," the woman says. "I knew your mother would be there and I didn't want her to be upset at you. You weren't hurting anything, not really. But there she was, huffing and puffing, and how could I not let her finish the job? I'm sorry now that I didn't speak to you. You must have misunderstood... Do you know, I envied her, climbing a tree like that without thinking twice. That's just what I liked about her, the longer l knew her—the way she just did things, and the devil get the hindmost."

This time she smiles with lips self- consciously pressed together, Nancy and Katherine both nod to her, and thank her for coming. When she exits, speaking to no one else, Nance notices how, even in this crowd she remains untouched, untouchable, frailer than she remembers.

"There is no accounting for the ideas that people get in their heads, is there?" says Kathy as the woman walks out. "Can you believe she said she actually envied Mother? Envied poor mama!"

❧

Nance will remember the syllables that night—Sylva Van Zant, the Countess, whose realm was the Odet women, and who ruled by their own decree. What a myth of cool elegance they had all three evolved, useful for lashing themselves for imperfection, she will see. And safe! Some royalty, trapped behind gauze curtains.

She will picture Katherine, pulling on gloves, still stuck at their girlhood table, longing for perfection—for perfection, momma! When what they were given was good, was better than most. A fierceness close to rage, this love she will feel, while she stares at the howl of the moon, remembering how she hated poor Katherine this afternoon, how she relished the thought of slapping her a good one.

❧

The next day, after breakfast, the sisters walk to the house where they grew up, the morning air still cool and damp, silent with sleep. For they still have the ashes to deal with; June Odet, their mother, has instructed them to scatter them behind the garden, near the hydrangeas she had planted. But someone else lives there by now; they feel like thieves, entering the yard.

Kathy says the place is so run down. How can they leave their mother there? How could they come to that place with their memories later on? God only knew how much worse it would be ten years from now.

Undecided, they walk along the sidewalk, around the corner, trying to discover between them what to do. And there is the house of Sylva Van Zant, the Chinese elm arching over the sidewalk.

"Here," Kathy says, on an impulse.

"Here? You can't be serious."

"I am serious. This place will always be beautiful. It's the place Mother most admired; she talked about it all the time, didn't she?"

"Yes, but not exactly—"

"—We don't have to tell the Countess. We could scatter the ashes here, under the elm. It would be done in a moment. Mother would like it here."

The lawn that sweeps back to the Van Zant home is emerald in the morning light, the air above it, hazy blue with moisture, alive with cicadas that click and shirr.

"We have a plane to catch and we have to do something. I'm not leaving her at that dump, with little kids digging her up playing trucks or something."

Nance is silent a moment. She pictures fighting with

Kathy about what her mother wanted, arguing that June Odet would probably enjoy the company. But it is Kathy who is alive, who must be lived with now, and Kathy is worried about appearances.

"All right," Nance says finally. "But you should say something. Say how much she means to us."

Katherine gives her a look, takes the container, removes the lid, peers in just over the edge, not able to look at the contents for long. Her eyes brim with tears, her face so red, she looks angry. She heaves a harsh sigh. "Here's to doing as we please, Momma. You tried to teach us that." Quickly Katherine tips the container and sprinkles the ashes around the trunk of the tree. "She'll be happy here," says the sister who is older and in charge.

⁕

On board their separate planes, the two women will think about what they have done, and decide separately that it was something their mother would have accepted. June Odet had lived a life in accommodation to what was imperfect, and somehow managed to be happy anyway, happy as anyone.

Katherine will be aghast at the way her eyes tear up every time she thinks of the moment again, of scattering the remains of her mother on the lawn of a neighbor she had not even liked. She will tell herself she is understandably overwrought, what with having to go home to more pressures on top of everything else. Always, everything, on top of everything else, nothing left over for herself. She feels so stuck.

But Nance will think again of her mother's big, sturdy body balanced in the crotch of the Van Zant tree, finished finally with her blustering, calling to Kathy not to be afraid—to trust her, let go now, Kath, and jump. And remembering her own gasp at the sight of Katherine's leap—there! above her, like she's flying!—will split that fleshy memory wide, so that Nance is sure in an instant that she and Katherine will talk again, sisters—sure and certain as one of her mother's avocado shoots opening the seed.

WORMS

The girl isn't yet twelve, and already she's skirting her mother's rule: no dating yet. He's only a friend, Caitlin pronounces to her grandmother, introducing a boy-colt in baggy pants, who ducks his head and grins in agreement.

Ann meets the girl's eyes, weighing the cost of confrontation in front of him. Rigid rules for such things are probably stupid anyway, she half-decides in the seconds it takes to survey the straight of his teeth, the large of his bones, the blunt of his fingers. They're just meeting some friends at the movies, Caitlin prevaricates; they do it all the time.

Caitlin's mother, Alex, is away at a conference, the girl entrusted to Ann a few days, and really, Ann thinks, she might as well try to resist the pull of the moon on the girl's tides. So much has changed, that she's unsure—and isn't age really more a matter of maturity than a ticking off of months? Besides, he's sweetly the gentleman. Caitlin seems strangely adult.

Ann nods her permission, waving them a good-time from the front door, excited and worried sick that she's been remiss in her gatekeeper duties. She'll report it to Alex and probably get scolded. Ann's own mother, long dead now along with so much else, had never relented on girl-rules, which were never broken in those days without consequences from God.

That world is gone, and so is Caitlin, gone off careless of what she knows little about. Ann defends against her mixed feelings, remembering Alex at that age, remembering her own stupid self at that crossroad. Has she ever told her Alex about how she'd sneaked past her own mother's iron rules with that damned cat? She's surprised to remember her crime, and to claim how badly it turned out, how horrifically splendid.

☙

Its kitten-beginning got found out in the tall grass of the orchard next to her childhood home. Ann's mother had believed animals belonged outdoors, same as young boys did, but Ann had smuggled it inside that summer and hid it in her room, until she discovered a sore on its neck, which to her horror had begun squirming.

She dropped the cat with a yelp and went running to confess to her mother, who, seeing the wound, gave Ann one triumphant look that said, You see?—didn't I tell you? She peered into the slit to open it wide. "Blowflies," she pronounced, and next plunged in a pair of tweezers to pull out a creamy white, living, squirming grub.

The sizeable, red, raw hole it left behind put Ann into shock at the scene: Mother pouring peroxide that foamed, kitten yowling. Ann had let the kitten go wild after that, the bearer of more than she was ready to know, its healing a miracle and also chance luck.

When you are young, she thought now in the living room of her grown daughter, thinking about her daughter's daughter, you turn away from the horripilations of life and the way living requires these—no, rather how life flourishes because of them.

Ann is as young as Caitlin in that memory, but the more experienced part of her argues that worms and grubs all perform goodly chores, eliminating tasty weak links, digesting garbage, cadavers. That's how life is, she'd just told Caitlin last night. She and the girl had watched that nature show on television, something underwater about the sex life of reefs and the jellyfish, who on a particular night each year, ruled by the phases of the moon, fill the ocean with their joined eggs and sperm, and sharks and barracudas come especially for the feast, gobbling gametes and jelly babies down.

Gross, Caitlin had said about the violent buffet and turned her face away. But these small disasters lurk everywhere—delicious.

The same summer Ann's kitten ran wild, before her youngest brother had been born, army worms had invaded her favorite climbing tree behind the garage. Ann hasn't thought of the tree since Alex was a girl. And now more worms? It seems too Freudian—

She stares out the window to where Caitlin just waved, wanting to connect some thread of herself to the girl, though the quince tree feels dangerous. Caitlin's glance, shy and in league with that boy, coaxing a smile from those soft lips of his, full of teeth—how long until she'd be home? Ann glances at her watch.

After Ann's mother had yanked out her cat's maggot, she became Ann's enemy, same as Alex was Caitlin's enemy now. A mother did what she had to do, Ann knew this by now, and as well that no daughter could love it.

She puts on music to soothe herself, but some
strain in the notes, a half-step of yearning for a minor key,
conjures up memories of her first girl-boy dance. Ann was
older than Caitlin then, and younger, because everyone had
been younger back then. Has she ever told Alex this story?
Has she even told herself?

Ann's best-friend, Jackie, had given the first party
to mark their sixth-grade graduation. Nothing about it
would have induced Ann to repeat it, but her mother and
stepfather, Vince, had helped chaperone at Jackie's, and it
was their idea to have Ann's first real boy-girl party. Ann
hadn't considered it her party so much as her doom.

The boys had lined up like bricks in a wall at Jackie's
house, flanking the tables loaded with boloney rollups and
bowls of rippled potato chips. They'd coughed down celery
stuffed with peanut butter, eyes empty of hope, mouths
drying shut. Not only did boys and girls not hook up in
those days, they stayed separate in a rule-filled romance
that was simpler and also more ruthless.

Ann had stayed across the room with all the other
girls, her rose-printed rayon dress crinkling whenever she
moved, her socks sliding down into patent-leather pumps.
She had chosen the outfit and had no one to blame for her
misery except for her mother, who had refused Ann nylons
and spoiled the whole effect.

Ann had wanted Tangee's "Natural" lipstick, too,
but her mother warned, once applied, it turned fuchsia
and cheap-looking, same as shaving your legs at too

young an age made you hairier and coarser, she'd pronounced.

Jackie's mother held fast against nylons, but had allowed Jackie the lipstick. Jackie slipped its metal tube out at the party, phallic as hell, dabbing it on her lips for the other girls to admire, first at her party, and later at Ann's. Putting their heads together, the girls had whispered and giggled to discover which boys across the room they found the least objectionable, the only way to view the situation back then.

Boys were never just friends, and the girls' loyalties to each other and their selection of boys could change positions like marbles in Chinese Checkers, transforming hues of opinion and outcome as quickly and thoroughly as Tangee and double-jumping.

Caitlin had told her it was different now, Ann thinks, though an ocean of sex still rolled, full of species previously unseen and amazing, the reason her stomach flips whenever she thinks of talking about sex to Alex, or worse, to Caitlin. Ann had wanted to escape those sure tweezers of her mother's rules, becoming the ocean herself, savoring those jelly babies and swimming, when, surprised, Ann recognizes her own mother had relished it, too, the excitement. Did Alex?

❦

All that summer Ann's mother had planned her party location. It had to be someplace superior to Jackie's basement recreation room. But their cellar was dark and smelly, and the living room narrow, their furniture overlarge.

The kitchen? The tiny dining room? Nothing seemed right. "If only I weren't expecting," Ann's mother had lamented; "I could find a summer job and rent you the roller rink."

How could Ann have forgotten for a moment that her mother was pregnant that summer? Ann had lost herself to Shakespeare, escaping. Her grandfather had given her a copy of the bard, and Ann took to riffling through bible-thin pages to ponder: What light on yonder window breaks? She practiced gliding her feet, sweeping her arms in what she hoped were graceful Elizabethan movements. Climbing into the low-spreading quince tree, out of sight of her mother, she brooded. Alas and alack.

A rusty oil drum stood on cinderblocks nearby, where Vince burned the garbage behind the garage, as people used to, another innocence of the time, Mother Nature thought forgiving. Surrounded by spangles of milkweed in bloom, Ann would sit in the branches, ignoring her mother's calls to come in and make her bed. At suppertime she would lie about her neighborhood travels and having gotten permission on the fly, arguing with her mother: Methinks thou forgetteth too easily, old crone. I was at Jackie's, hither and yon.

Ann's jump on the Chinese checkerboard of boys at Jackie's party had left her with a boy named Jonathan, not a terrible fate. He was a good enough baseball pitcher and had pale freckles to match strawberry blonde hair. Her mother said it was obvious: "He has a crush on you." Until Jackie's party, she and Jonathan had been unaware of one another, and then it became a painful awareness, a thing to be avoided.

Alex and Caitlin would laugh at her prudish naiveté, but for Ann it still seemed awful, climbing back to her memory perch in the quince tree, Hamlet's witches opened on the branch in front of her.

Jonathan had ridden his new bike up the cinder drive and knocked at the back kitchen door. When she leaned a bit, she could see him around the corner of the garage.

"Ann's out in the backyard," her mother gave her away. "She's watching her baby brother. Go look, and I'll get you something cold to drink."

Ann's face reddened, watching her mother turn like a great ship with her hull bulging out in front of her, one hand to the small of her back to tilt her pregnant bulk up the stairs to the kitchen. Her stepfather Vince liked to joke that it was her own fault for swallowing all those watermelon seeds, and her mother would give him a dirty look, saying, "Stop it, Vince!" Then he winked and warned Annie that she'd better be careful of what she ate, too.

Mother's voice sounded pleased about Jonathan, though.

"What are you doing all the way here?" Ann asked him, coming out from behind the garage. He was far away from home. He had to take the bus at school.

"You can go anywhere, if you've got yourself a good bike," he answered, patting the wide saddle of his new steed, impersonating someone careless about owning the newest luxury model, with a light, a basket, a built-in push-button horn.

They sat on webbed lawn chairs, Ann ignoring him pretty much, picking at a mosquito bite on her arm. "Is that your baby brother?" Jonathan asked.

She nodded, looking up to check on the two-year-old, who sat in the sandbox. Facing them, the toddler kicked his bare heels in the sand, shaking his hands out. He didn't like the sand when it stuck to him. He jutted out his chin at them, scowling.

"We call him Little Iron Jaw," she explained. "He doesn't talk much."

"You like to baby-sit?"

"No." Ann shook her head.

"Here we go," Mother called sweetly, bringing out three ice-filled metal glasses—turquoise, hot pink and pine green, on a metal tray she saved for special occasions. She poured them cherry Kool-Aid, handing the first drink to their guest. Ann peered down into her glass, drinking to feel cold on her upper lip. When she glanced up, Jonathan's eyes ran away, horrified by something behind her.

"Brucie, no-no-no-no*no!*" Mother said, reaching her arms out to her baby, who had yanked off his knit bathing suit, the flesh between his legs set free. He stood to pound his feet in the sand, crying, all of him wildly bouncing like jelly.

"Brucie, stop, no, you've got to keep your suit on, honey," Mother scolded, shaking the suit out. "Don't sit in the sand if you don't like the way it feels. Put your foot in here," she instructed, bending over to block their view.

Ann's weight fell into her feet. Her face burned, eyes lowered, turned away from her brother, turned away from Jonathan, whose mouth gaped, ringed with red, his cherry-stained tongue a wound she couldn't look at.

His freckled hands set down the glass on the rough picnic table. "I gotta go now," he mumbled, getting up. Kicking the kickstand, he pedaled straightaway.

"He didn't even finish his Kool-Aid," Ann's mother

moaned sympathetically, holding Brucie in the crook of one arm as she brushed the sand off her maternity top. "It's not your brother's fault," she added, sitting down with the baby on one hip, barrel stomach in the way. "He hates getting sand in his suit. Jonathan must know how that feels, getting sand on your wee-wee."

"Mother!" Ann protested, while Little Iron Jaw frowned, as if it were self-evident to him as well. Ann got up and ran toward the house, Mother calling, "Come back here and watch your baby brother."

"I've got to go to the bathroom!" Ann yelled to escape and remembers her relief at sight of her plain crotch: a wizened, smiling dolphin, squirting water, nothing jiggly.

How to ever tell Alex and Caitlin about this—when there was more? Days later, Jackie came to her house for an outdoor sleepover, and in those days, you'd put a blanket over the clothesline and weigh its edges with rocks to make a tent, and be thrilled about it. Ann has to re-imagine the whole world to believe her own memories: no clothes dryers, no campers with televisions, no Elvis on the Ed Sullivan Show yet, and no birth control, her mother proof of that.

Sex and education had not yet been combined in a sentence, and in those days, girls only heard rumors, or sometimes kabala-like words without meaning, only the sound of phlegm in the back of the throat, intended to appall: suck, fuck, cock, dyke.

Annie and Jackie lay with their heads near the blanket opening, looking out at the stars, excited to be near-grown up, lighting up scenery with the flashlight that Vince had leant them. They could have seen the stars more clearly if her mother had not insisted on leaving the bathroom light on to clear a path to the backdoor. She said that Jackie looked nervous.

"I'm not scared," Jackie protested, squeezing a pink plush cat to her chest when Ann's parents went back inside.

Jackie was the one who'd first told Ann in a whisper how babies got made. "You know the boy's thing? Well, he puts it in the girl's thing and that's what makes a baby, like planting a seed." Jackie couldn't say, "He puts it in the girl's thing," without placing both hands over her mouth, and giggling the giggle that Vince said sounded like a little machine-gun.

Ann at first believed this was another of Jackie's show-off lies. But her mother turned red as she stood behind her ironing board, when Ann told her about it and asked her to refute something awful and stupid.

Later Margaret would complain to Vince about Jackie's mom, unable to wait until Ann was in bed. That a mother would talk about that to her own daughter! No wonder Jackie was running wild!

So it was that Ann learned it wasn't watermelon seeds that had made her mother grow huge. It was a fate that apparently awaited Ann and all females she knew, a felt doom in her young mind that weighed heavily until she had a sensible insight into the matter.

On mornings when her family read the Sunday papers in bed together, Vince would yawn and stretch his arms out, pretending to knock the chins of Ann and her mother and little Iron Jaw, joking, like in the funnies: "Oof! Bonk! Oops, sorry! Not enough room in here." It was a small bed for two people, much less four. They all giggled and laughed. Still her parents insisted on sharing that bed.

⌘

"I know why our parents sleep together," Ann whispered to Jackie in the tent on their sleepover, having given this some private thought.

Jackie turned over on her stomach, putting her face close so as not to miss a word. She loved talking about things they weren't supposed to.

"They do it in their sleep. Nobody would do it on purpose, would they? So people who want babies have to sleep together because that's when it happens, while they're sleeping."

Jackie gasped, and then whispered. "When my cousin got pregnant? My mother said, 'You mean to tell me she's been sleeping with that Tarentino boy?' "

"You see?" Ann said, as triumphant as her mother had been with her tweezers, understanding the rules, feeling confident now. "That's why married people get double beds," she explained, adding about Jackie's cousin, "Only a dumbhead would go to sleep with a boy if she wasn't married to him."

"My cousin is stupid; my mother says she is."

Ann turned over on her back to picture a harmless, blind worm creeping through bedclothes to sleep in its fleshy nest. She cupped her hand between her legs, feeling its heat. Jackie was imagining something similar, because her plush cat and her forefinger came sliding under the sheets to poke Ann in the thigh, giggling. Ann giggled too, both getting louder, both pleased to be here in the tent together, wormless.

"Oh baby-baby, gimme a kiss," Jackie said, jumping up to press her lips against Ann's, laughing when Ann, heart pounding, pushed her away. Jackie always was boy-crazy, Ann's mother said.

❦

The same week her mother sent out Ann's party invitations, Ann went out to the quince tree to find its leaves moving, curling in waves like an ocean, or as if held to some flame, a phenomenon she'd experimented with at the garbage can. Up close, she saw hundreds of army worms, their green and yellow striped bodies, long and fat and undulating, rolling together.

Ann watched their palpitation, the rhythm of her lungs matching a muscular pounding at her center, exciting and frightening. She ran to get her parents.

"Good lord," her mother said when she saw it.

"I should have gotten them before they hatched. Now we'll have a real mess."

Vince said he'd seen webbing with some eggs earlier. He squeezed Ann's shoulder, knowing this her special hide-out, and then he lit a newspaper torch, holding it to the nearest branch. The worms curled tighter. Some reeled more wildly, standing up on their tiny last score of feet to wave their bodies like Shakespearean actors dying dramatic deaths.

❦

The tree's new unsightliness cinched her party's location. Guests had to use the front door to avoid seeing it, so the red couch went out to the garage to make space in the living room for dancing and a punch bowl. Her cat, gone wild, would soon have kittens in a box in that garage, its neck no longer a red, open wound. The wound was hers that night, filled with dull ache.

She remembers her mother's eye, overseeing, laughing and as fierce as some shark at a reef. The way mine might have looked tonight, Ann thinks, picturing herself in that moment of permission. She would try to tell Alex how sweet Caitlin's flirtation had been—Alex the mother who might even laugh too, eye teeth glinting—because wasn't that also a part of it?—life's ocean, jellied and jumping with gametes, swimming with jokes that could tear you inside out?

That night Jonathan had danced the most with Jackie, ignoring Ann at her own party. She had been left with a big blocky boy, whose name she can't remember now, only that his breath had smelled of baloney. And their two bodies had swayed in a slow-dance together, hands clasped, rocking in Elizabethan grace—Ann's appetites, the worms of her awful pleasures begun.

ACKNOWLEDGEMENTS

Thanks are due to those many publications that supported and encouraged my work, including a good many not listed here. Special thanks are owed to those who found room in their publications for these stories.

"Black Bears" was a finalist in Glimmer Train, Fiction Open, Top 25, 2008. It was published in Trivia: Voices of Feminism, www.triviavoices.com: Issue 13, Fall 2012.

"They Shout Praises" was first published in Other Voices 12, University of Illinois, Summer/Fall, 1990.

"In a House by the River" appeared in Louisville Review, University of Louisville, KY: Fall, No. 19, 1984.

"Goldfish" was published in A Room of One's Own, Canada, Vol. 26, No. 4, 2005.

"The Visitation" first appeared in The Writer's Bar-B-Q, Chicago: Issue 3, Fall, 1988.

"What Happened at Wanda's Place" was published in Kalliope, Jacksonville, FL., Vol. 9, No. 3, 1987.

"Walls" was published in Labyris, Lansing, MI: Vol. 4, No. 11, Winter, 1983.

"The Passing of McClusky" was published under the title "In Jeopardy" in The Sewanee Review, University of the South, Summer, Vol. XCIII, No. 3, 1985.

"Carpool" first appeared in Other Voices 5, University of Illinois, Spring 1987.

"June Odet and the Countess" was first published in Plainswoman, Grand Forks, ND: Vol. 11, No. 9-10, June/July, 1989.

"Worms" was published in Trivia: Voices of Feminism, www.triviavoices.com: Issue 15, Fall 2013

ABOUT THE AUTHOR

Rickey Gard Diamond's fiction ranges from short stories published in literary and feminist journals, to her novel, *Second Sight*. Published by Calyx and re-issued by Harper Collins, her novel was described by novelist Wally Lamb as "heartbreaking and life-affirming, serious and startling."

A journalist, Diamond edited the *The People's Voice,* Vermont's statewide newspaper on poverty issues, and was founding editor of *Vermont Woman.* Her series there, "An Economy of Our Own" won an investigative reporting award from the National Newspaper Association in 2012, and in 2015, she received a Hedgebrook Writer-in-Residence Award.

She earned her MFA in Writing from Vermont College of Norwich University, where she was later Professor of Liberal Studies for over 20 years. Her forthcoming book, *Screwnomics: How Our Economy Works Against Women and What We Can Do to Make Real and Lasting Change* (She Writes Press, April 2018), illustrated by cartoonist Peaco Todd, reframes the unspoken economic theory that women should always work for less, or better, for free. She lives and writes in Montpelier, Vermont, with her husband and their cat Azula.